EXODUS 20.3

Freydís Moon

Religious eroticism and queer emancipation meet in a claustrophobic monster-romance about divinity, sexuality, and freedom.

When Diego López is guilted by his mother into taking a low-key construction job in New Mexico, he doesn't expect to be the only helping hand at Catedral de Nuestra Señora de Guadalupe. But the church is abandoned, decrepit, and off the beaten path, and the only other person for miles is its handsome caretaker, Ariel Azevedo.

Together, Diego and Ariel refurbish the old church, sharing stories of their heritage, experiences, and desires. But as the long days turn into longer nights, Diego begins to see past Ariel's human mirage and finds himself falling into lust—and maybe something else—with one of God's first creations.

This book contains sexually explicit content which is only suitable for mature readers. Please be mindful: mention of transphobia, mention of drug use, light dubious consent (clarified via stream of thought), sexualization of religion.

"I do not say this lightly in any sense, but this was the most beautifully transcendent short story I have ever read. Immaculate writing, perfect tension, and a romance that gets threaded through our beings with every page. As a devotee of Southwest Gothic who is acutely aware of the role of the church in our everyday lives growing up queer in New Mexico, I proudly hail this short story as one of the most authentic and immersive examples of the genre and the experience of finding faith in places others would not dare to look. This tale means so much to me. I felt seen and heard and understood, but above all, I felt welcome. Thank you, Freydís, for telling our stories with such a raw passion and the very embodiment of freedom. I invite everyone to witness the miracle enclosed in EXODUS 20:3."

—R.M. Virtues author of *Drag Me Up*

"Freydís has created something truly exquisite in EXODUS 20:3. Their writing is lush, building the atmosphere into something both familiar and magical. The story is woven like a fever dream, drawing you into a world that feels so richly real one can practically feel the desert's heat and hear the church's floorboards creak. EXODUS 20:3 seamlessly intertwines blasphemy and holiness, with an eroticism that is sometimes subtle but always breathtaking. There is such sincerity in this story; from the start it grasps you by the hand and refuses to let go, leading you on a journey that feels both reverent and defiant. Reading EXODUS 20:3 feels like a religious experience, leaving you in awe by the end, wishing for more but also entirely satisfied."

—Harley Laroux author of *Her Soul to Take*

"Freydís masterfully combines the divine and mundane… Reading this feels like being anointed in something holy."

—Aveda Vice author of *Feed*

"At turns heartbreaking and hopeful, EXODUS 20:3 is a sumptuous tale of redemption, transformation, and the relationship between the erotic and the divine that will stay with you long after you finish it."

—Magen Cubed author of *Leather and Lace*

thou shalt have no other gods before me

Chapter One

"You have the address. Go."

Diego López gnawed his lip as he leaned against the rusted tailgate on his father's busted Chevy.

He cradled his phone against his ear and tried to focus on his mother's voice, exhausted and cold, rasping through the speaker. The gas station was quiet—nearly abandoned—but his attention darted to an oasis floating above the highway and a napkin tumbling across the empty lot. He pitched his shoulder upward to steady his phone and smacked a pack of Lucky Strikes against the heel of his palm.

"I can find a way to pay you back," he said and pulled a cigarette free with his teeth. "I don't need another handout, and I *definitely* don't need to play carpenter at some bullshit church to—"

"Cállate," his mother snapped. "You listen to me, mijo. You get in that truck, you drive to that church, and you make this right. No one put you behind the wheel of that car—*my car*—and no one put the... the *drugs* in your wallet, and no one—"

"*I know.*" He sucked smoke into his lungs and switched his phone from one ear to the other.

"This isn't about the money. This is about honor—*familia*. You go, understand? Go, work, get paid, come home. Do your community service and fix your life. This man, this Ariel, he's giving you a chance. Take it before he changes his mind and hires someone else."

"Yeah, because every able-bodied worker in town is trippin' over themselves to go rebuild a church in the middle of the desert, Mamá. Sure."

"You made your choice. *Go.*"

He angled his mouth toward the sky. She wasn't talking about his fourteen-hour stint in jail or the cash-bail she'd worked double shifts at the diner to pay for. She was talking about the sickle-shaped scars beneath his shirt, the choice he'd made three years ago—eighteen and able to say, *Yes, do it.* Same vague guilt trip, same acquiescence. *You're like a coyote,* she'd said to him once. *Halfway to a wolf but still something else.* He thought about that as she breathed on the other end of the line and imagined her sitting in the recliner in his childhood home, rolling a slender joint, watching fútbol while a pork shoulder braised in the crockpot. Sometimes she tripped over his name, her tongue unused to making the sound, but when she'd met him at the door after he'd been released from El Paso Detention Center, she'd said *Diego* with her full voice. Cracked every syllable like a bone.

"Yeah, okay." He sighed. "Do you want me to call?"

She huffed. "Eres mi sangre."

He shook his head and finished his cigarette, then crushed it beneath his boot. "Sé."

"Tomorrow, then. You'll tell me about the church?"

"Sure, yeah. Tomorrow."

"Drive safe," she said.

Diego ended the call without saying goodbye. He stood with his thumbs tucked through his belt loops. Endured the heat. Watched the road. Pictured himself elsewhere, across the state, settling in Austin. He'd bartend to make ends meet. He'd never touch narcotics again. He'd rent a studio apartment, and fill it with houseplants, and learn how to cook. He'd send money to his abuela, and he'd visit her more, and he'd grow the fuck up. Becoming another disappointment on the López family tree wasn't an option anymore.

It never had been, but stealing the car, *crashing* the car, getting caught... Yeah, that changed everything.

Early summer rippled through the dry air. He scanned his phone again, reading and rereading the address his mother had sent him—coordinates, actually—before he hoisted into the driver's seat and turned the key in the ignition. According to Google, Catedral de Nuestra Señora de Guadalupe was located in Luna County, New Mexico. He pulled his lip between his teeth again. Seven grand to help rebuild a decrepit church in the middle of the desert? Camming paid more. He'd found that out after getting hit with top-surgery bills. But now that his mother knew about the Vicodin, he certainly didn't need her to know about the porn too. He manifested the future he'd imagined—bartending in Austin, visiting his grandmother, making pozole in his apartment—and drove toward a city called Sunshine.

"Seriously," Diego whispered. He idled at the end of a dirt road, surrounded by cacti and hardy flora, staring miserably at a patch of graffiti painted across the front of the church. DIOS MUERTO covered the left door, and the word WALL, crossed out in matte red, filled the right. One window was missing, stained glass still hugging the frame. The roof slouched, but the steeple skewered the sky, crowned with a white cross.

He glanced at his reflection in the rearview mirror. Freckled brown face, piercing seated in the cushion where his lips bowed, eyes three shades darker than his skin. He was sculpted like his homeland, cheekbones high and chin round, eyebrows tapered and black. And he carried stubborn remnants of his childhood—long-necked and slender, wide-hipped and fine-mouthed—same as his tía. A bruise lingered on his jaw, planted there by a light-skinned cop, and gold glinted around his neck. Before he could squash the feeling, panic squirmed in his stomach.

Out in the middle of nowhere in his dad's beat-to-shit truck, hoping whoever needed a renovation assistant didn't *clock* him, and really, seriously, betting he wouldn't make it out alive if whoever hired him was—

Knuckles rapped the passenger window.

Diego startled, whipping toward the sound. *An asshole*, he thought, and then, *oh*.

A man peered at Diego over the edge of his sunglasses, eyebrows lifted curiously, mouth set and stoic. He was hard to gauge. Young, maybe. Or quite older. There was no way to tell. When he spoke, his voice was smooth and honeyed on the other side of the glass. "Are you lost?"

"I'm Diego—Diego López." He swallowed hard. "Are you Ariel Azevedo?"

"I am. You're here to work, right?"

3

Diego nodded tightly.

"Good." Ariel jutted his chin toward the church. "Come inside; I'll show you around."

Ariel Azevedo turned on his heels and made for the church. His collared shirt clung to broad shoulders, and Diego didn't realize his height until he pushed through the double doors, leaving them unsteady on their rusty hinges. He fiddled with his keys. *Huh. He's not what I expected.*

With his duffel slung over his shoulder, Diego raked his fingers through his short, black hair, dusted his palm over the shorn sides, and followed the path Ariel had taken. Silence fell over the desert, disrupted by distant cars and a barely-there breeze. A lone scorpion skittered beneath the warped panels at the base of the building. It was rugged—the atmosphere, the land, the job—and haunted, somehow. A place left to fester.

Diego stepped between the cracked doors and eased them shut behind him. Splintered pews cluttered the space, some of them toppled over, one split down the center. A rectangular fan whirled atop a cardboard box next to the pulpit, churning hot air.

"There's plumbing. The shower's stocked and clean, but no hot water," Ariel said. He flipped through an instruction manual and pointed with his pinky finger to an array of disconnected pieces on the floor. "Unfortunately, no air conditioning either, but I'll finish this before tonight, so you'll at least have a fan in your room. One bathroom, two adjoining bedrooms. Galley kitchen with a fridge and two-top stove. Generator is in the basement."

Diego gave a slow, thoughtful nod. He glanced from the vaulted ceiling to the dusty stained glass, assessing an image of the Blessed Mother rendered in gold and white. Candelabras clung to the walls, covered in dirt and grime, and a bowl meant for holy water sat bone-dry at the beginning of the aisle.

Ariel continued tinkering. He pushed cropped brown hair away from his brow. Dark, neatly kept stubble peppered his ruddy face, and his features were strangely sharp, as if he'd been cut from marble. Diego lowered his gaze to the floor.

"There's not much here, I know, but it's enough. Have you eaten?" Ariel asked.

He thought to lie, to say, *Yes, earlier*, but he shook his head. "Not yet."

"Your room is down the hall. There're fresh sheets, towels in the linen closet, curtains if you want them. Get settled, and we'll make dinner once I'm done with this."

The floor creaked under Diego's heavy boots. He tried to step carefully, avoiding areas that looked unstable, and paused in front of Ariel, paying mind to the scattered bolts and screws on the ground. "What am I here to do?" Work, yes. He understood that. But where could they possibly start in a place like this? It was an abandoned thing, incomplete and begging for demolition. He gripped the strap on his duffel, tipping his chin upward to meet Ariel's eyes as he stood.

Ariel furrowed his brow. He reached out and dragged his index finger beneath the gold chain around Diego's neck. When his thumb met the oval Saint Christopher charm, he pressed his thumb to the gilded surface. "Whatever I say." His voice was tender and coaxing, like someone speaking through bars, cooing at a caged animal.

Diego's breath caught. He stepped backward, eyeing Ariel skeptically, before he turned and walked toward the doorway in the far corner of the main room. His heart floundered. Heat pooled low, *low* in his stomach, and he thought, *Fuck. Who the hell is he?*

"Are you a man of God, Diego?" Ariel's voice carried, beating toward the steeple like wings.

Diego stopped. He drummed his fingers on the chipped doorframe. "Ask God," he said, tossing the words over his shoulder, and disappeared into the hall.

Chapter Two

Even post-sunset, Luna County burned. The night passed in sweltering increments inside the stuffy church. Diego slept with the sheets draped over his waist, bare-chested on a full-size mattress. The small repurposed bedroom had probably been utilized for storage in its last life. Now, it held a nightstand and a dresser, a tiny closet with shelves and a garment pole, and a skinny window facing the desert.

He'd dozed in fits, waking at the sound of footsteps after midnight, jolting upright as an odd hush whistled through the gaps in the glass. Prayer—spoken by the wind or a nomad—drifted into the room on a breezy whisper. Diego couldn't help but listen.

And the word was made flesh.

He snatched at sleep, lulled by heat and darkness, but hardly managed more than a few hours before dawn poured through the window. He blinked at the ceiling, searching for cracks in the slanted roof. A spider had strung a web in the corner. Dust clung to the sturdy beams. He reached for his abuelo's Saint Christopher, given to him when he'd been young and entirely different, and remembered Ariel thumbing at the etched icon. Like most unfamiliar places, Catedral de Nuestra Señora de Guadalupe had turned him restless. He felt childlike. Embarrassingly homesick. Still, he slipped out of the stiff bed, pawed at his eyes, and got dressed.

Across the hall, the sink ran. The toilet flushed. Diego waited for footsteps to come and go before he cracked open the door and walked into the cramped bathroom. He cleaned his teeth. Splashed his face. Raked texturizer through his hair. Stared at his reflection until his eyes wandered, settling on Ariel's toiletries—simple red comb, facial moisturizer, damp toothbrush. He touched the wet bristles and jerked his hand away, hyperaware of the awkward excitement thrumming in his veins. Such an intimate little tool, jammed into Ariel's mouth day after day. His voice rang in Diego's skull. *Whatever I want.* Confidence and curiosity. Abrasive, crisp syllables. Diego had never met someone like Ariel Azevedo; the immediacy of it pulled like a thread through his center.

Diego wasn't sure if he had a reason to be afraid, but he was.

"Are you awake?" Ariel's voice sounded on the other side of the door, followed by a light knock.

"Yeah—yes, sorry. I'll be right out."

"Meet me in the nave."

Nave? Diego pursed his lips. "Okay."

He checked his reflection, the tank loose on his narrow frame, blue jeans snug on his hips. He tightened the laces on his boots and searched the mirror again, shrugging on a thin flannel, concealing the tail-end of his scars. Maybe the fear was residual, prompted by instances every person like him tended to face in new situations. The what if, the potential threat, the worrisome undercurrent of being self-built. Lastly, he put on deodorant.

Noises echoed. Tools clattered, and heavy objects were pushed or pulled. He traced the outline of his phone in his pocket and walked into the main room—nave, whatever—to find Ariel, dressed in frayed denim and a white T-shirt, hauling items out of the building.

Ariel paused, midway in lifting a pew, and tilted his head. "Good morning."

"Mornin'," Diego mumbled. He pushed his fingers through his hair, a nervous habit. "What's on the agenda?"

"I need the nave cleared before we replace the floor. I assume you don't have a problem lifting? Your mother insisted you were strong."

"I'm strong enough," he said and nodded at a caved-in pew. "And the broken furniture? Are we breaking it down or fixing it?"

"I'd like to fix as much as we can." Ariel shrugged toward the open double doors. "Did you eat?"

"Not yet."

"Help me get this outside, and then we'll put some coffee on. There's toast too."

Diego curled his hands under the bench and lifted, easing forward while Ariel waddled backward. Outside, pews, chairs, and fixtures sat in the dirt lot, shielded from the sun by repurposed bedsheets.

Once they lowered the bench to the ground, Diego righted himself and cracked his back, scanning golden desert and hot stone. Last night, he'd shared the kitchen with Ariel, paying mind to each shallow cabinet Ariel opened. "Coffee, here," he'd said and pointed to Peruvian grounds, filters, sugar, and honey. "Pasta, ramen, frijoles, canned stuff. You're welcome to any of it. There're fresh vegetables in the fridge too. Juice, milk, soda—the works." Diego hadn't mustered the courage to ask for a beer.

"Hopefully, we can start on the foundation today," Ariel said. He set his hands on his hips, squinting at the displaced furniture. "Elena said you've done construction. Have you ever worked with laminate?"

"I've helped my dad with a few jobs. Nothing major, just framing and tiling. Some kitchen redesigns. Laminate's easy though. Shouldn't be a problem."

Ariel hummed thoughtfully. "And what made you decide to drive all the way out here for work?"

"My mother decided for me." Diego ignored how Ariel flicked his gaze from the horizon, shying under the careful once-over Ariel granted. He cleared his throat and swatted dust off his hands. "Coffee?"

Ariel nodded. "Eat too. You'll need your strength."

At that, Diego stayed quiet. Onyx rosary beads curved around the back of Ariel's neck, and red slid over his shoes as he walked through a patch of sunlight colored by a stained window. His age was still a mystery. His purpose too—what he wanted from this church, why he hadn't hired a larger crew. Diego had seen people like him in crowded malls, on busy streets, quiet and well kept, striking and unique, usually moving with purpose. Here and there and gone. Men like him, the secretive kind, usually made Diego wonder who he was meant to become. But this one, this Ariel Azevedo, tripped Diego's fight-or-flight.

"Grab the bread. There's apricot jam next to the egg carton," Ariel said.

Diego slid four slices into the toaster. "So," he tested, propping his hip against the counter. "What made you want to renovate this..." He shifted his gaze around the small kitchen, situated at the end of the hall adjacent Ariel's bedroom. *Shithole*, he wanted to say. "Place."

"Church," Ariel corrected. The coffee pot hummed and spat. He crossed his arms over his chest, watching Diego down the arc of his nose. "People need something to believe in, don't they? Señora de Guadalupe is the perfect opportunity to restore faith, inspire change, ease the disbelievers into believing in something holy again. In something higher and mightier than us."

"Restore faith, huh? In what? God? Heaven?" He slathered butter onto his toast, followed by orange-colored jam. "That'll chase poverty away? Extend visas? Tear down the wall? Because according to your front door, that's what *people* want."

Ariel took the sticky knife from Diego's hand. "Faith isn't a catchall, Diego," he said smoothly, as though he'd said *Diego* a thousand times. "But it's a comfort. Challenging, unruly, peaceful. Church gives us a place to worship, and worship gives us a chance to mend our wounds." Ariel dragged the dull knife between his lips, sucking away apricot jam. "You're wounded, aren't you?"

Diego paused midbite. "No," he said and bit through the toast. "Why?"

Ariel laughed, a single, quiet *hah*. Another once-over, quick as a snakebite. "I see it here." He pointed to Diego's eyes, then lowered his hand and prodded him gently in the chest. "And here."

"You always make assumptions about people you don't know?"

"Who says I don't know you?" Ariel's lips curved.

Ariel had shown nothing but matter-of-fact kindness, yet Diego still couldn't fucking breathe around him. Couldn't stand his elusiveness. Hated his ability to guard himself against intuition. For the most part, Diego got a good read on people. Like his own version of animal instinct—prey drive, primal understanding, wild perception—he usually dug to the root of someone within the first two interactions. Good, bad, somewhere in-between. Good enough to stick around and find out more, bad enough to turn and run, somewhere in the middle: hackles raised, teeth bared, standing his ground. Ariel gave him nothing though. Diego had no sense of who he might be or might've been. His heart skipped, anxiety swelling like a second skin.

Ariel's question echoed. *Who says I don't know you?*

Something hot and sharp crowded Diego's throat. He took a step back, putting necessary distance between himself and Ariel's hand. Before he could say *stop*, Ariel reached for his necklace again and

9

lifted the Saint Christopher charm toward Diego's chin.

"The patron saint of travelers, said to protect those of us who search," Ariel mumbled, eyeing the golden icon. His brows knitted, smile inching into a small grin. "What is it you're looking for?"

Diego swallowed hard. "Another chance, I guess."

"And what makes you think you don't already have that?"

"Mi familia no perdona," he said, too quietly. "One too many mistakes."

Ariel clucked his tongue and dropped the necklace. His gaze lingered on the bruise darkening Diego's jaw. "Let those who are without sin cast the first stone." He placed two fingers on Diego's chin, easing his face to the side. He dusted his thumb across the sore bruise. "Do you know the gospel?"

Diego nodded, frozen in place by fear or curiosity. The urge to shrink came and went, replaced by fervent defiance. To be seen, to be touched—these were desires he rarely entertained. But right then, he couldn't move, couldn't blink or lie. "Yeah," he said, the word gusting on a long-held breath.

"But I say to you, do not resist evil. If anyone slaps you on the right cheek, turn to him the other," Ariel said. "Do you understand what it means?"

"Turn the other cheek. Yeah, I get it—"

"Allow God to act on your behalf," Ariel said sternly. The side of his thumb caught Diego's mouth, flitted across the Saint Christopher, then dropped. "Make room for divine intervention."

"God has never looked out for me." Diego glanced at the two empty mugs on the counter and turned toward them, severing the channel between himself and Ariel. He filled both mugs and stirred cream and sugar into his own. Grasping the steaming top with his fingertips, he endured the heat on his palm, in his chest, deep in his center.

"It might feel that way, but whether it's God or one of his creations, you're certainly looked after. No one goes unnoticed," Ariel said.

Diego grabbed the other mug and handed it to Ariel. "If you say so." He snatched his second piece of toast and took brisk steps down the hall.

For years—an entire lifetime—Diego López hadn't felt the presence of a deity, a guardian, an *anything*. He'd been alone, stumbling through a childhood racked with confusion, landing in adolescence he'd tried to tear himself out of. He was just now beginning to understand what he had the potential to look like, sound like, feel like, and never once had he warmed under the attention of a greater being. At his weakest, he'd prayed; at his strongest, he'd prayed, too, but no one had ever made themself known. Not a devil, not a goddess, not *the* God. Diego had spent his life filling the silence with his own voice, rasping his vocal cords with cayenne and tequila and hormones until he finally recognized the sound.

Coffee burned his lips, scorched the roof of his mouth. He exhaled harshly and walked outside, welcoming the morning sun on his blushing cheeks.

Whatever Ariel thought he saw in Diego, whatever presence he thought Diego would feel, simply didn't exist. Faith was prescriptive, a placebo. Something brandished like a weapon in one breath and offered like a blanket in the next.

Diego fished a cigarette out of his back pocket and lit the tip.

"Those'll kill you," Ariel said. He'd arrived silently, like something with pawed feet, like something used to stalking.

"Why didn't you hire, like, a *crew* for this…?" Diego blew out a curl of smoke, shifting his gaze sideways as Ariel came to stand beside him.

"Didn't need one."

"You definitely need one."

"You're here, aren't you?"

"I'm not enough. What's your timeline anyway? When's this place supposed to be suitable for…" He sipped the cigarette. Exhaled. Laughed a little. "Worshippers, whatever."

Ariel was quiet for a long moment. His deerlike lashes cast thin shadows across his cheekbones, and his eyes were rich as soil, laced with honeycomb and amber.

Too beautiful, Diego thought. *Too perfectly made.*

"You're enough," Ariel said and set his coffee atop a covered pew. He nudged Diego with his shoulder as he swept into the church. "C'mon, we're losing daylight."

Diego drank his coffee, flicked his cigarette, and followed Ariel.

Get the job done, get paid, go home. The thought became a metronome. He tried not to think about Ariel's hand on his face, tried to ignore the thrum in his veins at the thought of being seen, of being excavated. *Get the job done.*

Diego worked until the summer heat crept under his skin, and then he stripped away his flannel and left it on the floor, wiped sweat from his brow with the back of his hand. When the sun was high in the sky, Ariel tossed his shirt in the corner of the nave, and Diego snuck glances at his bare chest, his hard planes and broad shoulders, smooth stomach, and lean arms. Brazilian, probably. Permanently sun-stained and ruddy like terracotta.

After he'd torn up the floorboards beneath a brightly colored window, Diego tipped his head back and caught his breath. As he stared at the ceiling, thinking *get paid, go home*, he saw Ariel in his peripheral, standing across the room, watching him inhale and exhale. Against the wall, sunlight pulled Ariel's shadow upright.

The dark patch spread outward, winglike and beastly, and when Ariel lifted his arm, raking his hand through damp hair, Diego swore the shadow bent, quivering like a nightmare.

Chapter Three

No, Mom, c'mon. I've got enough to cover my own food." Diego leaned against the front bumper on his father's truck, nursing a wrinkled cigarette. His mother hummed disapprovingly through the speaker. "Look, we're working on the roof now, okay? Should be done in a few weeks."

"It's been a week already."

"You're the one who signed me up for this, remember? No fue mi idea."

Another irritated hum. "And you still have money, yes? You're not taking advantage of the caretaker—"

"*Mamá.*"

"He's a nice man—"

"Ay Dios mío... Yes, he's very nice. I chipped in for groceries this week, and I'll keep paying for my half until we're done, okay? Relax."

Elena scoffed, laughing cruelly under her breath. "Now you have money, huh? Since when—"

"I'm hanging up."

"Mijo, don't you dare."

"Then *don't*," he hissed. He took a long, hard drag off the cigarette and blew plumes into the air. Exhaustion filled his voice. "Just don't, all right?"

Silence lingered. Finally, she spoke. "So, the church is moving along, then?"

"Yeah, Mamá, it's goin'. How's Leticia?"

"She's good. A little stressed from school, but muy bien."

"Good," he said, then again, quieter, "good."

"Call her sometime, okay?"

"Sí, haré."

"I'll talk to you later."

"Yeah, okay, bye."

The call ended, the absent *goodbye* lacking *I love you*. Diego swallowed around a jagged lump, stuffed his phone into his pocket, then sucked on his cigarette until the filter burned his fingers. The last five days had passed in a blur. He'd taken direction from Ariel—ripped up the floor in the nave, repaired the salvageable furniture, resealed the windows, replaced the front doors—and Catedral de Nuestra Señora de Guadalupe was beginning to look alive again. He gazed at the roof, eyes shielded by dark sunglasses, and watched Ariel climb a ladder propped against the side of the building. Afternoon sun bronzed Ariel's radiant, sweat-slicked torso. His rosary swung as he angled fresh shingles onto the slanted surface, trapping them with a nail gun. In the past days, Diego had found himself turning toward Ariel; his eyes had roamed rooms, looking for him. He'd jolted awake in the dead of night with a runaway heartbeat, listening to prayer float through the air, spoken by a voice—several voices—in languages he knew and didn't.

Diego feared him like a night terror, something he knew he could wake from if he tried. But the longer he stayed at the church, the more asleep he felt, as if he waded through the same dream day after day, chasing lucidity and never quite grasping it. The dream was always the same: Ariel at the edge of his fingertips, and Ariel saying words backward, and Ariel skewered with hollow bones, and Ariel pulled into different shapes. Feathers, falling. Eyes—jaguar, dolphin, human, goat—blinking. Diego on his knees, tasting salt and skin. The dream was always the same, and Diego felt Ariel like a hand around his ankle, pulling him beneath the surface of somewhere he'd never been. *I'm awake*, he thought, and crushed the cigarette under his boot. But while he worked, consciousness seemed to slip, and when he spoke, his mind felt suspended in lukewarm water.

I'm awake, right?

Desire had never knocked him the fuck out before, but he found himself apprehended—by Ariel, faith, belief in something, in anything. And he *wanted*—a stranger, a God, to believe.

"Hey," Ariel called, seated on the roof with his wrists flopped lazily atop his kneecaps. "Can you hold the ladder steady?"

Diego pushed away from the truck and loped to the church. He gripped each side of the ladder. "Okay, you're good," he hollered.

As Ariel placed his dusty boots on each rung, Diego glimpsed a displacement in the air. The space around Ariel's body throbbed, undulating like an aura. It shifted with his movements, fluttering outward from the center of his spine, floating like a helmet above his skull, there and gone in a blink. It dazed Diego, his chest weighty with anxiety, stomach flipped and knotted. When Ariel landed with a thud on the dirt, Diego swallowed around a woozy heatwave, trying desperately to shake away the feeling.

Awake, he thought, and reminded himself to breathe. *Get the job done, get paid, go home.*

"You're pale," Ariel said. He set his knuckles against Diego's forehead, then his cheek. "Are you feeling okay?"

"It's just hot," he assured. *I saw your wings.* "Need some water, I think."

"And something to eat. C'mon."

Ariel took him by the wrist, and Diego tried to slow his heartbeat, fixated on Ariel's palm snug around his pulse. In the nave, Ariel didn't let him go, and down the hall, Ariel didn't let him go. It wasn't until they were in the kitchen, and Ariel had guided him toward a plastic chair next to their makeshift table—an old, rickety patio set— that he took Diego by the shoulders and eased him into the seat. Diego tried to blink through the haze, listened to a cabinet squeak, to ice clank, to the fridge open and close.

"Drink," Ariel said and placed a cool glass in Diego's hand.

Diego set the glass against his parted lips. He relaxed as ice knocked his teeth and cold water soothed his throat. When he paused, Ariel curled his fingers around the bottom of the cup and tipped it toward him.

"Drink," he said again.

Diego opened his eyes, then his mouth. He drank greedily, hyperaware of the stream dribbling from the corner of his lips, over his chin, down his neck. He blushed horribly at the thought of Ariel holding the glass, sending water across his tongue, into his body, knowing the caretaker watched him swallow, paying mind to his stunted breath. Everything beneath his navel tightened, and Diego pushed his thighs together, eyelashes fluttering as Ariel swiped at the wetness on his chin.

When only ice was left, Ariel set the glass on the table. "Feel better?"

Reality tilted into place again, obscured, enhanced, but familiar. "Yeah," Diego rasped, nodding slowly. "Probably just dehydrated."

They ate cold chicken salad sandwiches with pickles and sliced tomatoes. Diego drank more water, then cracked open an amber bottle and nursed a skunky beer. Fans whirled in every room. The monotonous sound of their blades pulsed through the church. Hot air circulated, but summer was still oppressive, and the artificial breeze did nothing to shoo the fog behind Diego's eyes. He tried to distract himself, to think of something besides water on his chin and Ariel's heavy gaze, the otherworldly outline of appendages shimmering on the roof, and the tightness growing hot between his legs.

Being alone with someone, being close with someone, being contained with someone made Diego wonder about consequences. Made him consider opportunities. *What would it feel like to be with him?* He had fantasized about strangers. Bared himself for a quick fuck outside a gay bar in Austin, gone down on people in bathroom stalls and backseats, fallen into bed with acquaintances at parties. But he'd never felt like this before. Apprehended. Completely and utterly at someone else's whim.

Ariel scooped mustard onto his finger and sucked the digit clean. "Tell me about yourself."

Diego startled. "What…?"

"We've worked together for a while, and I don't know much about you," he said, filling a mug with steaming water. He added a teabag scented like bergamot and vanilla. "So, tell me."

"I…" Diego opened and closed his mouth, searching for something brave. Something interesting. Something true. *I'm the family fuckup. Total black sheep.* "I read a lot," he said. "Literary, mostly." *I've never been alone with someone like you.* "I studied creative writing before I dropped out, but I still follow free workshops online. I don't really…I don't really *do* anything, honestly." *I fuck myself on camera sometimes.* "Work odd jobs, you know. Like this one."

"Odd jobs," Ariel parroted quietly, as if he knew better. "Why'd you drop out?"

Diego rubbed his fingers together. "Big price tag on education."

"American dreams are expensive, querido."

Querido. Heat rushed into his face. "That's what we come here for. Land of milk and honey, no?"

Amber eyes flicked around his face. "No," Ariel whispered, shaking his head. "Just the land someone took. Tell me about your odd jobs."

"I bartend."

"And?"

"Construction, obviously."

"Obviously," Ariel mumbled and rested the mug against his bottom lip. "And?"

Words wedged like a stone in his throat. Diego tried to swallow, but everything burned brightly, eagerly, as if he had no choice, as if Ariel had reached into his mouth and hooked his finger around the truth. "I've cam'd before. I don't have a big following or anything, but I've got a few loyal subscribers. Low-key stuff. Nothin' extravagant."

Ariel tipped his head. "You sell yourself?" he asked. Kindly, somehow. Politely.

He laughed under his breath. "No, I sell *videos* of myself. Sometimes I livestream too. I know that's not exactly godly—"

"You mean biblical?"

"Excuse me?"

"Biblical," Ariel repeated. "I doubt God would take issue with what you do or don't do with your body. The Bible was written by men— torn limb from limb and poorly sutured by the kings of Mysia. As much as I cherish the Gospel, it isn't exactly *godly* anymore. Holy, yes. Important, yes. Inspirational, yes. But it's the Bible that condemns promiscuity. Not God."

What a strange thing for a man like you to say, Diego thought. He tilted his head, mirroring Ariel's previous motion. "Aren't you…aren't you, like, a pastor or something?"

"No. I'm someone with an idea. That's all."

"Uh-huh. And rebuilding this church is your *idea*? Restoring faith?"

"Yes, and providing access."

Diego finished his beer. "To God?"

"To faith. People don't lose faith, Diego. They're forced away from it. Ostracized from the very fabric of it. This place can change that."

"I don't know if I believe that, but I'm glad you do. Someone should."

"Why is it hard to believe?" Ariel sipped his tea and met Diego's eyes. "You pray, don't you? You ask for forgiveness, you try to make amends, you ask for direction. What's the difference between faith and tenacity?"

"Results, I think," Diego said. "I've prayed, yeah, but not in a long time. Maybe that's my problem." He leaned on the back two legs of the chair, stretched out his arm, and dropped the empty bottle in a blue recycling bin. "Maybe God can't hear me."

"I doubt that," Ariel said.

The desire that'd struck through Diego when Ariel had placed the chilly glass against his mouth lingered. It was a bowstring, pulling tighter as the evening deepened. He wanted another beer, but he couldn't convince his legs to move; wanted fresh air but couldn't fathom leaving the table. This strange, powerful man had him snared, caught like an animal with its foot in a noose.

"What about you, then? Cuéntame," Diego said.

"¿Le dirá qué?"

"¿De dónde eres?"

"Lençóis. Very small town in Bahia."

"Brazil? I thought so."

"What gave me away?"

"Your accent, for one. You've got that Portuguese annunciation," he said, then made a soft *chuh* sound. "Not border-Spanish, not Mexican Spanish, not fast-lipped Chilean Spanish. It's easy to spot."

Ariel hummed, nodding. "And you? Where are you from?"

"El Paso, born and raised. Mi familia es de Guanajuato. Parents are here, grandparents are there. How old are you?"

At that, his mouth split into a shy grin. "Why?"

"Humor me," Diego said.

"How old do you think I am?"

"Thirty."

"Good guess. How old are you?"

"Twenty-one."

"You're young," he said reverently.

Diego steeled his expression. Young, maybe. But he'd fought against the world, against himself, to live long enough to become *Diego López*. Surviving a traitorous body, an unstable mind, and an unenthusiastic family made his quaint two decades feel a lot longer. He gave a curt

18

nod and averted his eyes, scanning the plastic table. Wind rattled the roof and pushed hard against the small building, caused the windows to quiver and the doors to flex. It was a frightening thing, being in the middle of nowhere with someone who paid attention. Who *saw* him. Who listened.

"When's the last time you prayed?" Ariel asked.

"When I got locked up." He expected resistance, questions, judgement.

Ariel simply nodded. "And if I asked you to pray with me tonight, would you?"

"Maybe." Diego cleared his throat, considering. "Yeah, I would."

Ariel stood. His chair scraped the floor. "Get cleaned up. We'll pray before bed."

Diego didn't move until Ariel crossed the hall and stepped into his bedroom. He blinked, turning over the last few hours in his mind: the fragmented light splintering away from Ariel's body, wing-shaped, radiating like armor; the water behind his teeth, on his chin, following the length of his throat. Truth pulled from Diego by a force he didn't recognize—unearned trust or sainthood or something worse.

What gave me away?

Fight-or-flight resurfaced and prodded Diego in the chest until he stood, unsure if he should slink into his bedroom and lock the door or go along with whatever Ariel had in mind. It was prayer, wasn't it? Just prayer. He could handle that.

In the bathroom, Diego brushed his teeth and scrubbed his dirty skin with tea tree soap. He smoothed coconut lotion over his legs and arms, rubbed shea butter on his fading scars, and strung his Saint Christopher around his neck, staring at his reflection until footsteps filled the hall. He touched the piercing on his lip, then the patchy stubble on his jaw, and made a mental note to shave in the morning.

"Diego," Ariel said, his voice echoing through the church.

Diego dressed in nightclothes—gray joggers, ratty white tank—and padded barefoot into the nave. The floor was scratchy and naked, torn apart from rough work. Soon, laminate boards would fit over the filth, covering the old, unkempt foundation. Ariel stood where the pulpit should've been and laid a bath towel on the ground.

"Kneel," he said with the weight of a basic command.

19

The air shifted and everything paused as if the cracked baseboards and empty space held their breath. Diego took hesitant steps forward. He watched Ariel from beneath his lashes and lowered to his knees. Something new and impatient yawned inside him, akin to desire, abrasive and unhinged. His bones were like busted pipes, hunger gushing through his fractured skeleton. He swallowed hot saliva as Ariel knelt before him, carefully removing the rosary from his neck.

"Give me your hands," Ariel said.

Again, Diego obeyed. He lifted them, paying mind to the fine tilt of Ariel's mouth, the awkward bend of his lengthy fingers, and exhaled sharply as smooth beads wrapped around his knuckles. Ariel pressed the crucifix into Diego's palm and sealed their hands together, shackling his smaller, scarred digits in an iron grip. Diego stared at him, wide-eyed and unblinking. His heart thundered. That woozy, dazed feeling returned, and he remembered to breathe. *Inhale, exhale.* He tried and failed to ignore the spasm between his legs when Ariel squeezed him.

"Lord Jesus, at the Last Supper, you knew Judas, one of your sacred twelve, would betray you," Ariel said.

Diego couldn't recall the prayer, but appropriate words tumbled out all the same, fed to him from somewhere, by someone. "Deliver us from false friends and treachery."

"Close your eyes," Ariel whispered, then continued. "There, our Lord, you washed the feet of your disciples."

"Make us meek and humble." Diego saw light cross the blackness on the backside of his eyelids. Tendrils moved and curled, undulating like snakes. He gripped the rosary hard, honing on a separate sense: Ariel's calm breath, his warm voice.

"You gave us the Sacrament of your body and outpoured blood."

"We stand in reverence before the——" Diego sucked in a trembling breath. "——the eternal…" Smooth, slender fingers slid past the waistband of his sweatpants, but he felt Ariel's hands wrapped around his own; he knew the shape of Ariel's boyish thumbs and strong palms, keeping him still. There was no possible way for Ariel to be in two places at once, yet the touch was deliberate, invisible fingers slipping between his thighs, tracing the soft curls around his cunt. "Ariel——"

"Eyes closed," he said gently. "We stand in reverence before the eternal…"

20

Diego's jaw slackened. "Covenant—eternal covenant," he said, body flushed and trembling.

"You asked your disciples to pray with you in the garden."

"Keep us awake and watchful." His knees shook, spine bowing as the phantom touch grew more insistent, framing his swollen clit, diving downward, rubbing tenderly where he was wet and open.

Ariel spoke evenly, each word coasting across Diego's cheek. "Lord, at the time of your arrest, at the moment of your betrayal, your friends fled."

"Give us…" Diego swallowed, fumbling with the rosary. "Give us courage in times of trial."

"You were falsely accused and condemned for speaking the truth."

"May we choose honesty in the face of injustice," Diego said weakly. His lips quaked. He wanted to understand, to say *stop*. No, *don't stop*. To open his eyes and be face-to-face with the man who'd turned prayer into promiscuity. But he didn't know if Ariel was responsible. If it was him or a divine force or if Diego was losing his mind. Soft skin pressed against his stomach—wrist, forearm—and whatever was touching him leaned closer, pitting him like a peach. He was too afraid to open his eyes. Too enraptured. Instead, he widened his legs and silenced a pitiful moan.

"In the courtyard, Simon Peter swore he did not know you three times." Ariel dug his fingers between Diego's tight knuckles, absently plucking at a rosary bead.

"Make us faithful in times of…of temptation," Diego choked out, enduring confident, slow strokes to his front wall.

"Pontius Pilate handed you over for crucifixion."

"Have mercy," Diego gasped out. His lower half throbbed, coiling into heated knots. "Have mercy on us sinners."

"You were beaten, mocked, and humiliated."

"May we suffer…" His voice cracked, broken by a whimper.

"Gladly," Ariel supplied.

"*Gladly*. May we suffer gladly."

"On the cross, you were taunted, and yet you forgave."

Fuck. Another finger pushed inside him, sinking deep alongside the first two. "May we always live in…in…"

"Obedience."

21

"Obedience," Diego blurted. His body relented, giving over to the pleasure pulsing in his groin. His cunt clenched and spasmed. Everything below his bellybutton tightened. Shockwaves traveled into each limb, causing his hands to jerk and his body to go rigid. He breathed like a runner, like someone in the midst of escape.

"From the cross, you promised paradise," Ariel cooed. He coaxed the rosary free from Diego's hands, toyed with his trembling fingers, and followed the lines on his sweaty palms.

"Make us long for eternal bliss." Diego sighed.

The ghostly appendage removed itself, leaving him slick and empty. He wanted to crumble into a heap, strip away his clothes and babble through another prayer. Beg God or Ariel or whoever had been inside him to use him like a whetstone. But when he opened his eyes, Ariel was easing backward, and Diego dropped his hands into his lap.

"See," Ariel said. "God provides."

For a moment, Diego considered agreeing. His mind was humid, fogged with *yes* and *please* and *again*, but reality registered, came to him in starts and stops. There he was, kneeling in a church, half-fucked and flushed from nose to toe. There he was, on display, completely and utterly *known*. He stumbled to his feet and made for the hall, glancing over his shoulder as wobbly legs carried him to his bedroom. Whatever had just happened, whatever had been done to him, he'd wanted it. Encouraged it. Prayed for it. And he didn't know how to feel about Ariel Azevedo witnessing it or…or influencing it…or…

"Jesus *fucking* Christ," Diego whispered. He twisted the lock. Raked his hand through his hair. Paced from the window to the door, again and again. Waited until the hall light clicked to take a deep, audible breath.

He couldn't think. Couldn't sit still. Certainly couldn't sleep.

In all his life, he'd never experienced something like that—unhinged desire, pleasure from an unseen place. He wanted to reach into his mind and uproot the memory, rip it out, and bury it. He couldn't close his eyes without thinking about Ariel's voice, and he couldn't get comfortable without rubbing his thighs together, reminiscing on how he'd convulsed around an invisible hand. And he couldn't divorce his thoughts from *more* and *now* and *need*. Hours passed, and his skin still burned, and his heart still quickened.

At midnight, Diego propped his phone on the windowsill, angled it toward the bed, and crawled out of his clothes. He livestreamed for a little while. Rested his chest on the mattress and shoved a pillow beneath his hips, fingering himself hard and fast. He ground shamelessly against his palm, lifted onto his knees and worked his knuckles deeper, panting through another white-hot orgasm. Satisfaction was fleeting. Diego caught himself fantasizing about a bottle inside him, about someone's fist or an oversized toy. He whined and twisted himself in the sheets, ashamed and hot and taken off guard at the thought of a cock jammed down his throat, wishing someone would fuck him until he cried, gagged, *hurt*. He tried to envision gentleness. Soft touches and lovemaking, but the imagery didn't stick.

At two o'clock, Diego pulled on his joggers, grabbed his pack of smokes, and tiptoed through the church. The air was mild outside, clinging stubbornly to heat, and the white moon glowed above the desert. Stars formed a patchwork across the clear sky, suspended in the blackness like dew on a spider's web.

Diego leaned against the side of the church and lit his cigarette. Smoke filled his lungs, prodding at his tightly wound muscles and lessening the anxiety worming under his skin. The world felt dreamy and unordinary. Fuckin' upside down. He tipped his head against the building and exhaled. He was tired enough to close his eyes, to drift as he let the church take his weight, nursing a cigarette and listening to footsteps creak on the unfinished floor inside. A door opened. Dirt and pebbles crunched.

Ariel sighed, a relieved noise. "Those're bad for you."

Diego opened his eyes. He couldn't parse this particular reality. Couldn't peel back the layers and decide if he was trapped in a dream or awake and exhausted. He flicked his gaze around Ariel's angular face. Beautiful, same as most Brazilian men. Wild though. As if he actively tried to blend in. Diego understood cloaking and masking in his depths, knew the range and restraint it took to perform as something palatable, something redeemable. He lolled his head against the wood paneling and sent smoke into the air.

"Am I awake?" Diego asked.

Ariel stepped closer. "You tell me."

"And if I'm not?"

"Then you must be dreaming."

23

He finished his cigarette and flicked it. Orange embers skipped across the dirt. "And if I am?"

"It's your dream. You dictate what happens next."

"Do you think we're seen here?"

"By who?"

God. Diego didn't answer. He didn't have to. Tension ratcheted, and the night thickened, gorgeous and expansive and deserted, a space carved out for them, for this, for whatever they'd started together. His throat worked around a swallow. He stretched out his hand and looped his finger around Ariel's knuckle. Anticipated a collision. Crashing; combusting. But Ariel eased toward him, crossed the minuscule space in a single step as if his boots hadn't touched the ground, like his body had transferred from there to *here*. Near enough to taste his breath, to watch his chest stutter and his eyelids droop. *You dictate what happens next.* In the distance, a coyote yipped. Closer, Diego loosened the reins on his self-control and framed Ariel's face in his palms.

"Do you see me?" Diego asked.

At that, Ariel's mouth curved. "Sí, querido. Te veo."

Do you want me? Diego wasn't brave enough to ask. Instead, he stood on his tiptoes and pulled Ariel into a clumsy kiss. He hadn't expected resistance—not in his own goddamn dream—but Ariel shied away, their lips disconnecting with a soft, familiar sound. The first thing Diego thought to do was apologize. He couldn't move, though, couldn't speak. Fear turned him to stone. He pressed himself backward, sealing his spine against the church, and blinked, inhaled shakily through his nose. When he finally convinced his body to react, Ariel swooped toward him again and seized his mouth in a deeper, harder kiss.

Like lightning, Diego López was emancipated, freed completely. He gasped between Ariel's parted lips, tasted mint and copper on his tongue, felt a strong grip cuffing his waist, his ribcage, his waist, his ribcage, both at once. He inched his fingers into Ariel's dark hair and clung to him. Head spinning, heart running, he kissed greedily, like it was his last meal, like he'd been teased with something worth taking. Swallowed raspy, encouraging moans sent into his mouth on hard-won breath, exhaled like a blessing. A nip at Ariel's lip earned a harder grip—*yes*—and a thigh wedged between his legs—*yes*. He thumbed at Ariel's cheekbone, his temple, and brushed across smooth, feather-like material—skin, not skin—speared through with bone or needle. Opening his mouth for another hungry kiss, Diego tracked a palm skirting his sternum, fingernails scraping his side, knuckles tracing his joggers, a palm resting heavy on his lower back. *Impossible*, he thought, and then, *nothing is impossible in a dream*.

Diego broke away to breathe, to go to his knees, to make a demand. *Touch me. Take me. Use—*

But he stopped. Blinked. Shuddered through an exhale. "Ariel," like *wait*, like *don't*. It was too late though. The moment Diego opened his eyes, he saw the diamond-shaped orb peering at him from Ariel's forehead. Feathers shooting away from his skull. Appendages outstretched, littered with eyes. Human, goat, leopard, reptile. Diego blinked, just once, and heard wings beat, feathers cutting through the night. In the midst of his lashes flicking, Ariel disappeared.

Diego braced against the church and turned his gaze skyward. *I'm awake*, he thought, and hiccupped through a soft, surprised laugh. *What are you?*

Chapter Four

Sunlight tossed a kaleidoscope around the nave, streaking the newly laid laminate in different colors. Diego had woken with a start, jolted upright in bed, pawing at his chest, feeling across his throat, clinging to the hopeful delusion that last night had been real. That he'd been awake—truly awake. That he'd gone to his knees with Ariel and prayed, and came with a hand wedged inside him, and licked into Ariel's mouth under a starry sky. Diego had blinked and caught his breath, still damp between his legs. He took a shower to clear his head. When he'd checked his earnings, the livestream session had brought in four hundred and ninety-six dollars. Seven comments had read *MORE*, three others had read *louder pls,* and one had said *that's it bitch keep squirming for me*. He'd wrinkled his nose at the half-assed, faux-dom demand. But somewhere buried deep, in a place he didn't dare look, Diego liked the safety of it. Sometimes being demeaned by a username, someone he could attach a made-up identity to, made him wetter, made him come harder, and that *always* raked in bigger tips.

Last night happened, he assured himself. *It did, it did, it fucking did.*

Diego had eaten microwaved oatmeal and drunk orange juice straight from the carton. He'd shuffled around the church, accompanied by silence. Outside Ariel's bedroom, he'd stood listening for sounds of life, and decided to get to work after hearing nothing but the fan. Keeping his hands busy would put his mind at ease, at least. So, he focused on the floor—cutting the door jams, spreading the underlayment, placing the planks—until morning bled into a dusky afternoon, and tires chewed through the dirt lot outside. He paused with his hands curved around a plank. A car door shut, and boots stomped the rocky ground. Diego refocused on the flooring as Ariel walked inside.

"Hey," Ariel said, curt and polite. There was a bag tucked under his arm and a six-pack dangling from his bent knuckles. "I had to run an errand. Grabbed lunch while I was out." He jostled the paper bag. "Burritos, chips, the works."

Diego bristled at the sight of him. It was an animal reflex—looking at Ariel, remembering last night, smelling frijoles and meat and lime. He stood clumsily on the cusp of disbelieving his own memory. Imagined Ariel with a third eye open between his coarse brows, steady and unblinking, the same way it'd been fixed on him last night.

"Thank you for getting started," Ariel added, filling the awkward quiet. He gestured to the half-finished nave with the six-pack. "Are you hungry?"

"Starving." Diego swallowed the rest of what he wanted to say: *what are you, what did we do last night, what do you want with me, can I have you?* "I didn't know you liked beer."

"I'm not a nun." Ariel avoided the fresh laminate and stepped over Diego's spilled tools, then walked briskly into the hall.

Diego snorted. "Yeah, I'm aware," he called, wincing at the sound of his brash voice bouncing toward the eaves. Abandoning the plank, he trailed Ariel into the kitchen, tempered the heat in his face, and tried to calm the fluttering in his chest, like a thousand moths bouncing against his heart.

"Pick," Ariel said and pointed at two foil-wrapped burritos.

Diego took the one labeled SPICY LENGUA and dug in the bag for plastic salsa cups. He found pickled veggies too. "Can I have one of those?"

The bottlecap came away with a *snap*, and Ariel's fingers grazed his skin. He pressed the beer into Diego's palm, offering a meek smile. "I don't know what you usually get, but I figured you can't go wrong with..." He waggled his fingers at the table. "...chicken and beef."

"You weren't wrong." Diego took a swig from his beer. He leaned against the unstable table and dunked the corner of his burrito into chunky green salsa.

They ate in each other's company, filling the silence with mastication and gurgling sips. They sucked sauce and grease from the sides of their hands and stole glances at messy mouths. Last night lingered— the dream, the truth—tilting beneath Diego's skin like loose water.

27

He finished his lunch, then his beer, and lowered into a plastic chair, studying the dirt on Ariel's laced boots.

What happened last night? Diego tested the question in his mind, but when he spoke, "When do we need to be finished with the renovations?" came out instead. He licked his teeth and dug his thumbnail into the center of his palm. *Coward*, he thought, scolding himself. *Fuckin' pussy.*

Ariel scrubbed his mouth with a napkin. "I'd like the first service to be on August fifteenth," he said, nodding contentedly. "The Assumption of Mary."

Diego tipped his head, furrowing his brow.

"It's the day the Blessed Mother ascended into heaven, reborn as her holy self, assuming her role in the high kingdom as the earthly caregiver of the Son of God," Ariel said.

He tossed the napkins and litter in the trash can and grabbed two more beers out of the fridge. After uncapping both bottles, he shrugged toward the nave. As he walked, Diego followed closely behind him, listening. "Technically, scripture doesn't suggest that Mary lived and died a human life. Some believe she simply left this plane for a different one; others believe she was immortal. There's interpretive theology around it all—thoughts and hearsay and Catholic campfire stories. But regardless of who-says-what, the Assumption of Mary is still an important date for many people. A bridge, so to speak. Mary lived a blessed, difficult life. She faced trials before entering paradise—became acquainted with grief, knew suffering, witnessed poverty and betrayal. I don't think there's a better day to open Catedral de Nuestra Señora de Guadalupe. Do you?"

"A church named after the Blessed Mother, opening on the day she ascended into heaven? No, I think that's pretty fitting," Diego said and took the beer Ariel handed him. He tipped the bottle against his mouth just enough to wet his lips and licked the skunky flavor away. "What's next?"

"Finish the floor, fix the furniture, paint. That's it." Ariel heaved a sigh, surveying the half-finished nave with a slow, steady sweep. "Do you think we can manage that in three days?"

"Two if we're quick."

"Good. Then let's be quick."

Diego snatched the unlaid plank, slid it into place, and hammered the edge until it sat flush with the one beside it. He drank his beer slowly, internally flinching at every hard *smack* of a tool, *bang* from a plank, *crunch* of a handsaw. Ariel worked swiftly, moving around the church with efficiency Diego still wasn't used to. Every movement made sense. Each turn of his hand and gathered breath and sturdy step was meticulous; precise in a calculated, inhuman way that made their kiss—dream or not—seem outside his realm of possibility. The way Ariel had surged toward him. How he'd been vigorous and hungry, fitting himself into Diego's rhythm. That version of him didn't match what Diego saw right then, what he'd noticed since the first day he'd arrived.

But Ariel *looked* at him. Shifted his eyes toward Diego like a wolf watching a deer, like a hunter watching the hunted. Like Diego was a twenty-point buck, and the wolf was weighing his options. Like Diego was something sharp, and the hunter was counting his bullets.

It made him feel extraordinarily powerful to be looked at like *that* by someone like Ariel.

Powerful, but uneasy.

They worked well into the afternoon. Ariel left his shirt bundled on the floor next to the tool case, and Diego tossed his tank into the hall. Sweat left his skin shiny, his pink scars standing prominently against his copper skin. At one point, he righted himself and sat back on his heels, wiping his brow with the back of his hand.

Ariel cleared his throat, cutting another quick glance along Diego's body. "What're those?" He asked the way most people who already knew the answer asked, politeness giving way to curiosity, hoping for an interesting answer.

"Double lung transplant," Diego said sarcastically. "Brutal, man. Total bloodbath."

A soft laugh bubbled up and out of Ariel.

Diego caught himself thinking, *Laugh more. I like the sound.*

"Well, you have a…" He paused to clear his throat. "I was going to say beautiful, but I don't know if that's the right word."

Heat unfurled behind Diego's sternum. "A beautiful what?"

"Body. I like what you've done with it."

Diego stifled a surprised laugh. He turned toward the window, shielding his bewilderment. "Oh," he blurted stupidly. "Beautiful is a strong word, but it's not…it's not *bad*."

"Or wrong?"

"Depends on who you ask."

"You don't think you're beautiful?"

Diego finished pounding one of the last planks into place. His stomach turned to ribbons. Air thickened in his chest, and his skin became feverish, unused to acknowledgement. Typically, he fucked in the dark. In shadowy alleys outside crowded clubs, a wandering hand crammed in his pants on a neon-lit dance floor, tumbling around a bed with nothing but moonlight skating through the blinds. No one called him beautiful and meant it. Sometimes *handsome*, mostly *hot*. Whenever *beautiful* had been used, it'd been tit for tat. Praise for an act during a livestream session or left in a crude comment beneath a purchasable video. *Come for me, beautiful. Show me agony, beautiful. Lick my boots, beautiful.* He never deleted them, but he never read them more than once either.

He didn't know how to answer. Not really, at least. Not honestly. "I don't…" He struggled through an awkward laugh. "I don't know."

"You are," Ariel said matter-of-factly.

"I'll take your word for it." Diego stood, trying to shake off the tightness pulling his skin closer to his skeleton. He felt seen again. As if Ariel had yanked back his ribs and peeked inside. "We should let the laminate rest overnight before moving the usable furniture back inside. Should probably tape and tarp for paint too."

"If we paint tomorrow, we can have the furniture assembled and placed on Saturday. We'll finish with a day to spare, like you said."

Diego nodded. "We haven't missed anything, right? The roof is done. Public bathroom is remodeled, windows are solid, walls are patched. Anything else?"

Ariel hesitated, shifting his weight from foot to foot. For the first time, Diego saw his hand twitch, watched his throat flex around a nervous swallow. It was a slow thing: Adam's apple bobbing, neck elongating. He parted his lips but didn't speak for a long, calculated moment. "There's one more thing," he said. Caution guarded his eyes and filled his voice with an unsure rumble. "I can trust you—can't I, Diego?"

The question held weight. He considered it, thinking *no*, thinking *yes*, and remembered the shock on Ariel's face after they'd kissed last night, how his inhumanness was abrupt and unexpected, as if Diego had called it to the surface without realizing. He toed at the smooth floor, watched Ariel breathe and blink, and finally said, "Yeah. Can *I* trust *you?*"

"Yes." Ariel turned and strode into the hall. "C'mon, I have something to show you."

At first, Diego didn't follow. He stood rooted in place, waiting for wings to sprout through Ariel's back, feathers to cover his skull, eyes to stare out from hidden places. But Ariel didn't change, he just paused in the mouth of the hallway and glanced over his shoulder expectantly, prompting Diego to step forward. *Ask*, Diego thought, again and again. *Ask, ask, ask.* And then, *Demand. Make him tell you the truth.* But what *was* the truth? That Diego had imagined being touched last night? That he'd thought about Ariel while he fucked himself for an audience? That he'd dreamed about the church caretaker and imagined him as something impossible? Diego inhaled sharply, trailing Ariel through the basement door next to the bathroom, down a set of wooden stairs. An exposed bulb buzzed to life, illuminating the dingy space, filled with sacked flour and plastic-wrapped cots, water jugs, and clean linen. Diego turned his eyes from the washer and dryer against the wall to Ariel, waiting for a clue, an explanation. Something, anything.

"Nice basement," Diego said and lifted his brows.

"Do you know how long it takes to walk from here to Chihuahua?" Ariel asked.

He blinked, taken aback. "Mexico? Like, forever, I guess? A day at least? I don't know. Why?"

"Just over fourteen hours. Two days, seven hours each day. Three days, four and a half."

"And...?"

Ariel lifted the edge of a ratty Persian rug thrown across the floor and rolled it away, revealing a hatch built into the floor. He huffed through a sigh, eyes heavy on Diego, before he unfastened the lock and pulled the door open. A short ladder, propped against the inside wall of the tunnel, led to a dirt foundation.

Reality struck Diego, fast as a rattlesnake, and he caught himself tripping through surprised laughter. "You..." His smile stretched into a grin. "You're a coyote," he said, hushed, like a secret.

"No." Ariel lifted his gaze, staring at Diego through his lashes. "But I need a coyote."

Diego cinched his eyebrows. He tilted his head, glancing from the tunnel to Ariel, back to the tunnel, back to Ariel. The pieces slipped into place inch by inch. A rundown church, renovation that would've taken two days with a full crew but took longer with a single work-for-hire, Ariel's constant reinvention of faith, of boundaries, of bridges. Diego blinked several times. He reminded himself to take a breath. "You…you want me to…?"

"It isn't free work, Diego. You'll be compensated. I'll take care of you. But I need someone I can trust, someone who understands, and—"

"You realize I crashed my mother's car into a light pole, right? Got caught with Xanax, Vicodin, Oxy? That's the reason I'm here—make enough money to cover what my mother loaned me and start over somewhere new. I…I have a record, Ariel. You can't seriously expect me—"

"I expect nothing," he said. Gentleness warmed the disappointment swelling in his voice. "I only ask that you think about it. There're two other safe houses on the tunnel route. An animal sanctuary just outside the border and a homestead near Sunshine that belongs to the same family who owns the taquería where I got our lunch today. I spoke to them about the technicalities—payment, safety, timing—and we came to an agreement. The only thing I need is a man on the ground."

"A *coyote*," Diego said, snapping at each syllable. "If I get caught, I'll go to prison—"

"You won't *get* caught." Ariel snapped too. Elegantly. Like he'd perfected the art of persuasion.

Diego rolled his bottom lip between his teeth and chewed. His mind whirled, tossing scenarios around—handcuffs around his wrists, blue and red lights flashing, people running—but his thoughts were cut short by the suddenness of Ariel's hand on his jaw, cradling his chin.

"I will keep you safe," he said again, his voice low and baritone.

Everything faded—fear, anxiety, helplessness, curiosity, thrill—until the only question Diego had left came skidding out, whispered and raspy, like something mistaken. "Did I kiss you last night?" He swallowed hot saliva and cleared his throat. "Did we—"

"Yes, we did."

He expected relief, but anger spiked through him. Anger and excitement and ferocity. "What…" He made an effort not to close his eyes, leaning into the tender pass of Ariel's thumb dusting his mouth. "What *are* you?"

Ariel's eyes scaled his face. He dropped his hand and tapped the Saint Christopher charm centered between Diego's collarbones. "Something that can keep you safe," he said and walked away. His boots thumped on the stairs.

Diego listened to each footstep and sent a prayer into the tunnel at his feet. "Quédate conmigo," he whispered. *Be with me. Give me answers.* "Darme respuestas."

Chapter Five

At midnight, Diego lay awake, listening to the box fan spin in his bedroom. After standing in the basement, reciting prayers to himself, he'd grown too nervous to pay attention to his stomach and had gone to bed without dinner. He'd left the door unlocked, hoping Ariel might appear after dark. But hours had passed, and the church was still quiet. Completely unmoving, stifled by the desert heat. Diego turned onto his side and stared at the doorknob.

Something that can keep you safe.

The fine hair on his nape stood. He drummed his fingers on the pillow, watching the dark strip at the base of his door. He willed something to happen, but nothing moved, and no one approached. Stillness remained, flexing with every inhale and exhale. As he breathed, he considered his own humanness, his entire life, and wondered about potential, about recklessness, opportunity, and power. What could be more powerful than unstitching an oppressive system? What could be more reckless than sliding out of bed, and opening his bedroom door, and walking into the nave?

He pushed his soles into the newly laid laminate. Glanced around the tall, open space. Moonlight tilted off the image of Christ etched into a stained window and glowed on his thorny crown. Another box fan spun in the corner, circulating the dry air.

Get the job done, get paid, go home.

Something like fear radiated inside him. He closed his eyes and held his arm out, palm open, waiting for Ariel Azevedo to appear. Maybe he would, maybe he wouldn't, but Diego had to *try*. He couldn't say no to the job—a scary, hard, dirty job—without knowing who and what he was walking away from. That cousin to fear, that ripe thrill and aching anxiety, knotted so tightly it hurt to breathe.

"Show me," he said to no one, to Ariel, to whatever God might be listening. He squeezed his eyes shut. His outstretched arm trembled, the other clutched close to his chest. *Please*, he thought, prayed, demanded. *Please, show me.*

Something small and soft touched his palm. Landed there, as if it'd floated toward him from the ceiling. Diego opened his eyes and found a pearlescent feather, spotted rusty-beige at the root, seated in his hand. He dragged his thumb along the feather, watching it ripple and split. His heart skipped. For a moment, he forgot to be afraid, to be thrilled, to be anxious, until he realized his body was trapped in a shadow, until he heard lungs expand, until the silvery glow coming through the windows behind him defined the shape looming at his back.

"Don't be afraid," Ariel said. He sounded like himself and not. Like several versions of Ariel had spoken at once.

Diego froze. His pulse raced, but he kept his eyes wide, staring at the darkened hallway as movement echoed through the church. Feet against the floor. Disrupted air. A sound like machinery humming, an engine purring. His lips wobbled, gaze shifting upward to take in the magnitude of wings—*fuck, wings*—spreading outward from Ariel's reshaped body.

Ariel landed in front of him, and Diego recognized his rich, brown skin. But his lungs still malfunctioned at the sight of *him*, at his long torso fixed with arms, four of them, and his legs, jutting forward on bony, equine knees, split at the shin where hooved appendages settled on the floor behind his humanesque heels. His face was elongated, exquisitely sculpted, and breathtaking. Feathers fanned over his skull. Scales the color of abalone flecked his temples and crawled along his fae-like ears. The diamond-shaped eye in the center of his forehead didn't blink, but it quivered, shifting to take in Diego. The rest did too. Eyes nestled between feathers, peeled apart on Ariel's slender wrists, and took the place of his bellybutton. His hollow cheeks carved open, showing white teeth, sharp in all the wrong places.

Ariel's voice filled the church. "See me."

Diego tried to stay upright, but his ankles gave way, and his legs buckled, and he crashed to his knees, gazing at a horrifying miracle, at something completely impossible, at God's first creation. That tippy, woozy feeling resurfaced, the one he'd succumbed to during their prayer session, the delirious, eager *want* that'd coaxed him outside, into a dream that wasn't a dream. "What're you doing to me?" he asked so quietly he could hardly hear himself.

"Seeing *you*," Ariel said. His molten eyes burned through any reluctance Diego had left. Ariel stood tall, his dual-wings—one smaller pair sprouting from the back of his ribcage—curved toward Diego like a shield. "You've been given choices, Diego López. Your submission is offered freely, is it not?"

His muscles tensed at the word *submission*. Still, he nodded. "You didn't... When we prayed, you didn't give me..." Diego paused to breathe, to glance around at different eyes. Some familiar, most of them not. "You didn't give me a choice."

"I gave you opportunity," Ariel said. His voice ricocheted, so deep, so low. "And you took it."

Diego blushed terribly. It was true. Cruelly so. When they'd prayed together, Diego could've opened his eyes, he could've said *wait*, he could've said *stop*, but he hadn't. He'd known Ariel was touching him, somehow, and he'd allowed it. Enjoyed it. Encouraged it. Wanted it again, right then. "Tell me what you are," he said as evenly as he could.

"I am duality." Ariel's wings trembled, eyes fluttering between spotted feathers. *Like a falcon. Like a predator.* "Designed in the image our creator manifested before the beginning, when the universe was still an ambitious idea. Where you are made of stardust and recycled matter, I was created in the likeness of the canvas you were born to decorate—lightness, darkness." His mouth was still his, parting delicately for each word. "Sentinels guarding Earth, shepherding *you*."

Diego's shoulders loosened. Everything inside him said *run, stay, don't, yes*—a cacophony of contradictions. *Yes* bellowed loudest. "You..." He stared at Ariel's dual arms, his long, bony fingers. "You touched me," he blurted, trying and failing to stop his head from spinning, his blush from worsening. "Why...why did you...?" Nothing made sense. Not the insatiable want coursing through him, not the celestial being standing before him. "Why me?"

Ariel leaned toward him, cradling Diego's jaw. Slender digits framed the top of his throat, and Ariel tipped his face upward, baring his neck. "You are my golden calf, Diego López. You have remade yourself, rebuilt your own empire from within, and demanded recognition from the world. Reverence from unbelievers. Now, tell me, what did you come here for?"

"Absolution," Diego said, and it was the truth.

"Then you've come to worship?"

"Yes," he choked out, nodding against Ariel's palm. A fire raged in his abdomen, between his legs. "Tell me what to do. Please, *please*— tell me how to worship..." *You.* "Tell me...or...or show me."

"Worship is a choice. A gift." Ariel unfurled his wings from their place across his lower body, exposing himself to the biblical depictions in the windows, and the crucifix propped in the corner, and Diego, on his knees, unhinged and malleable. He brought Diego closer, guiding his mouth to the dual cocks hardening between his thighs. Ariel's smaller, slender cock curved toward the eye where his bellybutton should've been. Beneath it, the larger, heavier shaft jutted toward Diego, wet at the tip and flushed like a plum.

Desire writhed inside him. He waited for revulsion. Waited for *flight* to take a hold and send him running to his father's truck. But all he felt was an insatiable want—to please, to worship, to be held and seen by something godly, by someone beyond him. He opened his mouth for Ariel's thumb, scraping his teeth along the prominent knuckle, and when Ariel pulled his hand back, he dragged his lips across too-hot flesh.

"Only if you're willing," Ariel said gently, on a shuddering breath.

God, he was. The determination of his own will frightened him. He took Ariel into his mouth, laving his tongue along smooth, salty skin, and reached for the smaller cock above, learning the shape of him in slow, tight strokes. There was no comparison for this. No way to anticipate what was or wasn't good. Diego did what he knew how to do—loosened his jaw, hollowed his cheeks, let his throat constrict and his eyes water—and moaned around the strange, sulfuric taste of a new body.

Ariel palmed the back of his head, and Diego relaxed his slippery lips, flinching through a wet gag as Ariel held him in place. The sound was animal and sexual, his throat rebelling, his tongue going rigid, his stomach leaping. Diego made a wounded noise as Ariel slid deeper, stringing saliva onto his chin, causing his cunt to squeeze around nothing. He'd gagged on plenty of dicks before, closed his eyes and allowed his mouth to be abused, his cheeks to be struck, but he'd never choked on the slow, sensual pull of someone easing into him, tickling the sore bloom at the back of his throat. No one had ever treated him tenderly when he'd whined, when tears had slipped down his face, when he'd slackened his jaw and swallowed. But Ariel touched him gently, running his hand over Diego's head and thumbing at his damp lashes.

The moment Diego pulled away, Ariel let him go. He braved a look at the angel standing over him. Three eyes—two brown, one gold. Several more watched from his wings, some glistening, others rolled backward. The reptilian eye at Ariel's navel wept, and Diego licked at the tears—sweet, like syrup—before he wrapped his lips around the second cock.

Slow, he reminded himself, and relaxed for the hot, deep press crowding his throat. It was easier to take than the first. Diego suckled at the base of Ariel's cock, his hairless pelvis flavored like maple tears, and let his throat flutter and flex, his tongue push and knead.

Ariel held him there again, rumbling like a beast. "To what extent do you wish to worship?"

Diego shifted backward. He rested on his heels, breathing hard. "What're you willing to give me?"

"Whatever you want."

"What do *you* want?"

At that, Ariel paused. Two of his hands came toward Diego, cupped his damp cheeks, ran along his clavicles. His quad-wings shook, the two larger appendages stretching behind him while the smaller duo folded against his sides. "Worship is obedience." Ariel slid a pair of fingers into Diego's mouth. "It is acquiescence and deliverance. Acceptance. Will you give me that?"

Diego nodded, biting lightly. *Will it hurt?*

Ariel's fingers slipped free. *Will you hurt me?*

In a different scenario, Diego would've gritted his teeth and embraced pain. But there, with Ariel, someone otherworldly and out of his depths, he couldn't fathom a worthless fuck. The thought of self-punishment delivered through Ariel's angelic body turned his stomach.

"Don't hurt me," Diego said instead. One boundary set.

Ariel purred in agreement. He offered a hand, which Diego took, and helped him to his feet. Everything seemed slower, hazier, as if he'd entered a separate plane. Somewhere close to the surface of sleep but awake enough to be dangerous. Like he'd sipped wine for hours or was fending off the tail end of an edible. The fraction of the world they occupied was thick and heady, and Diego wanted to stay there. He left his joggers in a pile on the floor and stood before Ariel, bare and willing.

Light shimmered around Ariel, shaped like elongated orbs. They phased in and out of view, shifting like an aura. He took Diego by the shoulders and turned him toward a patch of moonlight puddled on the floor. "Show me how you pray," Ariel said. "On your knees, head bowed."

Diego pushed his thighs together and did as he was told. Bathed in muted white light, he went to his knees and curved his chin toward his chest. It wasn't until Ariel gripped his nape that Diego thought, *oh*. Not until he was guided to the floor, his blistering cheek pressed to the cool paneling, did he realize what Ariel had asked of him. He laid his palms flat on the ground, opened his legs, and closed his eyes, swallowing around embarrassment. *Touch me*. He wanted to push backward. *Touch me, touch me, touch—*

The side of Ariel's palm slid between Diego's thighs. Pleasure burst inside him; broke like an overripe berry. He keened and arched, gasped and panted. He'd never been so raw before, like there was a livewire loose inside him. Like he'd been playing on the edge of an orgasm and was too keyed-up to come. Fingers rolled across his swollen clit and then sank inside him. His hips reared toward Ariel, but the hand on his nape tightened; another hand gripped his ribs, *another* settled on his hip. He was bound. Kept completely still while Ariel stretched him. He heard the sound of his body opening, whimpered and grunted as Ariel drove his hand deeper, and gasped when Ariel pulled away, inching a slick digit into his ass.

"Wait—*wait*." Diego shot his eyes open, breathing fast. "We need—"

"Don't doubt me, little coyote." Ariel's voice—*voices*—careened around the church. A sound like laughter, like a drum or a heartbeat, came and went, and something hot and wet landed on Diego's tailbone.

Diego felt it again: slow, oily dripping. He searched his peripheral and caught the blurry outline of Ariel leaning over him, saliva stringing from his mouth, coating his rim. Diego let his eyes slip shut, reveled in the obscurity of it. This. *Them.* He braced for another slow, steady touch and willed his muscles to relax while Ariel prepped him. One finger, two. Three. Whatever had been in Ariel's mouth served its purpose. The sting lessened, the discomfort faded, and Diego babbled with his face against the floor.

"Please," Diego whined, knuckles whitened. "Please, Ariel. Por favor, ten piedad."

Have mercy.

Catedral de Nuestra Señora de Guadalupe remained quiet, burdened with breath, and the flutter of Ariel's wings, and a strangled gasp Diego couldn't control. Ariel was careful, methodical, but he plunged into Diego on a single, fluid thrust, filling him entirely. The movement was unexpectedly primal. Diego's head swam. *Fuck.* His throat ached, but he made hoarse, pitiful noises, enduring the suddenness, the overwhelming heaviness. Ariel moved slowly, shifted his hand from Diego's neck to his skull, threading his fingers into his hair. He sank deep, *deeper*, until his hips were flush against Diego—smaller cock buried in his ass, larger in his cunt—and rested there.

"Again," Ariel said, strained as if he'd spoken through set teeth.

"Ten piedad," Diego whispered, panting. "Please, please."

"*Again.*"

"Mercy," Diego choked out. "Have mercy on me, Ariel. Please. Let me...let me come. Please. I—"

"You're here to worship," he said matter-of-factly, "are you not?"

Diego's lashes fluttered. He swallowed hard and tried to nod. "U-use me," he croaked. "Use me, please. Be gracious. I'm..."

"You're what, Diego?"

He exhaled a sharp breath. "I'm yours—I'm *yours.* Just...just please—"

Ariel cut him off with a strong thrust. He released Diego's head and braced two palms on the floor, caging him there. His other hands latched around hipbone and meaty thigh, holding Diego's smaller frame steady. It was sex, and it wasn't. Primitive, instinctual fucking. The kind tagged "breeding" on Pornhub. Deep, rhythmic movements. Clapping skin and stunted breath, one body splayed beneath the other, submitting completely. It was sex, and it was something else. Diego hadn't given into the idea that worship could take different shapes, that he could be *worshipping*, could be giving himself over to a deity. But he was.

Soft, boyish noises slipped from Diego's lips. Ariel remained quiet, breathing and humming like an engine set to idle. Even when his pace quickened, hips snapping harder, grip tightening on Diego's waist, he hardly made a sound. Diego hadn't anticipated the deep-set heat, hadn't prepared for his muscles to seize and his body to stiffen. He'd been entranced, pleasure-drunk and overworked, and his orgasm shocked through him. Woke him. Caused his eyes to widen before they shut, his brows to knit and his knuckles to bend. Ariel gasped too. Diego felt him still, heard his hitched breath and predatory hiss, and wanted to silence himself, wanted to halt the yelp echoing through the church, wanted to smother his clumsy cries and shaky moans, but he couldn't move. He couldn't do anything except endure, and give in, and go sweetly limp.

Ariel kept Diego on his knees and fucked him in earnest until he followed suit, coming on a low growl. Warmth flooded Diego, liquid and moving, and he thought it might not end. Thought Ariel might spill over inside him. Thought, *am I crying?* And realized, yes, those were tears on his cheeks, and yes, that was Ariel running down his thigh, and yes, he was awake.

No dream could've compared.

The showerhead sprayed lukewarm. Water formed rivulets down Diego's body, running across his drooping shoulders and weak legs. Sweat and soap and come circled the drain. It was different—whatever angels carried inside them—clearer than he was used to. Hotter too. Everything about Ariel was warmer than most. His skin, his eyes, his voice. Diego blinked through a sleepy fog and tipped his head back, welcoming water on his face. It'd be morning soon, the last morning before the church reopened, and he had no fuckin' idea what to do. He thought of Austin again. A new city, another chance, a different life. But after tonight, after doing what he'd done, the dream he'd hoped to make a reality paled in comparison to the mystery he'd found at the church. How could he leave Ariel Azevedo after worshipping him? After seeing him naked and ancient? He *was*

ancient, wasn't he? Diego sighed, thumping his forehead against the shower wall.

"What the fuck are you doing?" he said to himself as he squeezed more shower gel onto his palm and gave his body another scrub. Soreness gathered behind and below his hips, an achy throb where Ariel had been. His knees were scuffed and bruised too. Throat scratchy and battered.

Little coyote.

Those words surfaced repeatedly, and Diego hated the exhilaration they brought. The purpose they hinted at. The chance at something beyond him, bigger than him, floating just beyond his fingertips.

I will keep you safe.

The water was losing what little heat it'd had to start with. He turned the knob and stepped out, dried off before he pulled up his briefs and walked into the hall. Darkness spanned, deepening in the direction of the nave, and ribboned with lamplight around Ariel's closed bedroom door. Diego almost crept into Ariel's personal space to ask to be held—something he'd never done before. Usually, he left or watched someone else leave. If he ever stuck around postcoital, it was for mediocre cuddling: an arm thrown over his waist, sloppy kisses pressed to his shoulder, *that was good* mumbled to the sound of a zipper raking, clothing shuffling, bathroom stall unlocking. He'd been held by a girl once, a long time ago. His high school sweetheart. She wore a lesbian pin and enthusiastically *loved him anyway*, and he thought about her in equal parts bitter and sweet. It opened like a pit inside him—thinking of being held, wanting to be held—and he found himself knocking shyly on Ariel's door.

The door opened while his fist was still raised. He startled, dropping his hand, and blinked, unsure of what to say. It seemed childish, standing in his briefs, lonely and a little confused, still trying to piece together what he'd done. What they'd done together.

"Can I sleep with you?" Diego asked—because that was the question, right? He scrunched his nose. "*Do* you sleep?"

Ariel looked human again, but a shimmery oasis clung to him, shaped like pointed ears and wings and extra limbs. Now that Diego had truly seen him, he couldn't *unsee* him. Ariel's mouth ticked upward. He stepped aside and held the door with his foot. "I sleep," he said, like a parent to a child.

Diego walked into the simply adorned room. Ariel's bed was pushed against the wall, draped in a fluffy white comforter. A crucifix was nailed above the window. The curtains, pinned away from the glass, showcased the desert—stars, moon, silhouetted cacti—and a desk, littered with tattered books, sat opposite the bed, forcing the foldout closet to remain permanently open. A discarded shirt hugged the leather rolling chair, and a lost moth beat against the lamp bulb, fluttering frantically until Ariel cracked the window and shooed it outside.

"Do *you* sleep?" Ariel asked.

Diego sat on the edge of the bed. He waited there for a heartbeat, then two, and shifted backward, lying with his back to the wall and his head propped on a crooked elbow. "Sometimes."

"Sometimes," Ariel echoed playfully. He slid into bed next to Diego and gazed up at him, lulled like a sun-warmed lion.

"You owe me an explanation," Diego said.

"Ask whatever you'd like."

"Are you an angel?"

"That's a man-made word, but for all intents and purposes—yes," he said and dragged his knuckles along Diego's arm.

"How old are you, really?"

"Thirty *was* a good guess, but honestly, I'm not sure. Older than this place though."

This place. An entire planet. Diego swallowed his discomfort. "When you look like this…like…"

"Human?"

"Yeah, human. Is it a spell or—"

Ariel laughed. His fingers found the curve at Diego's waist and settled there. "It's evolution, I think. I've been living with humans long enough to mimic your mannerisms, your appearance, your fragility. That's what happened after the Fall. We learned to adapt, to cloak ourselves, but sometimes the mirage is hard to control. Hard to keep intact."

"You fell…?" Diego braved a touch to Ariel's stubbled jaw.

"Yes. Most did, at least. We're alike, us and you, both seeking an absent father."

Diego tucked his arm close to his chest and laid a cheek on the pillow. "So, if you're an angel, then there's a God?"

"There's a being beyond us. God? Maybe. Whoever it is, he's a creator I can hardly remember." Ariel's minty breath coasted over Diego's mouth. "That's why so many of us fell, landed here, became gods in our own right. People needed hope—still need hope—and we're able to provide that."

"Sounds a lot like blasphemy," Diego mumbled.

"An idol is only false if veneration ends at the idol itself. Those who seek us out pray *through* us. We're conduits for worship, not usurpers."

"Why not show yourselves, then? Why hide?"

A touch to his chin. "People would call us monstrous. You know that."

Diego hummed, unconvinced. "And you..." He inched closer, tapping his lips against Ariel's chin. "...fuck out of wedlock, I guess?" he asked, smothering a bout of laughter.

Ariel laughed too. Raspy, handsome laughter that made Diego blush. "Believe it or not, some of us are convinced *you* were made in *our* image. Pieces of you, at least. Like God took what he'd already accomplished and perfected his design." He brought their bodies closer, ghosting a phantom palm across the scar under Diego's pectoral. "And yes, we do fuck." The curse chimed like a bell. "Some of us more often than others."

"What about you? How often do you screw the hired help?"

"It's been a while."

"Awhile?"

"Years."

Diego quieted. Lowered his gaze to Ariel's mouth and memorized the shape—sweeping curves, plush and full—completely, unequivocally entranced. He looked for a long time, stared at Ariel's fine, pretty lips, and hoped they'd find his own.

"You'd like to be kissed," Ariel said as if he'd solved a puzzle.

Diego furrowed his brow, confused. "You seem surprised."

"It's rare. Only a few species kiss."

Diego's blush worsened. "Do you like it?"

"I like it enough. Do you?"

"Yeah, I do," he whispered and swallowed nervously. "But it's not... it's not—"

44

Ariel kissed him. It was a sleepy, clumsy kiss, but it made Diego's chest ache all the same. *I'm kissing an angel,* he thought, and closed his eyes as Ariel pressed his lips to temple, forehead, cheek. *I'm in bed with an angel.* Ariel turned over and swiped at the lamp string, bathing the room in darkness. When the angel faced Diego again, fingertips traced patterns on his tailbone, and feathers draped across his skin, tickling his shoulder.

Chapter Six

Diego held his phone lazily, tipping the image of Leticia to-and-fro. Her unruly curls were freed from the braid she usually wore, face bare except for a shock of red lipstick. She snapped a pink bubble at the screen, chomping like a truck driver.

"Mom's still pissed," she said. The gold hoop punched through her nostril caught a stream of sunlight, momentarily blinding the camera. She adjusted her phone and sighed. "What're you doin' out there anyway? She said you're rebuilding some dumbass church."

"That's pretty much it, yeah." Looking at his sister was like peering into a time warp, seeing himself unmade in a parallel universe. He sat back in the clean pew and glanced around the freshly refurbished nave, which still carried the chemical scent of paint and orange oil. "See, look." He tapped the screen and moved his phone from side to side, shifting the camera to the polished pulpit, neatly arranged pews, sparkling candelabras, and a golden dish half-filled with holy water. "Not bad, huh?"

"Damn, wow. I thought she was makin' shit up."

Diego flapped his lips. "Whatever. How's school?"

"Oh, it's hell," she said, barking out a laugh. "But I'm gettin' through it."

It felt like just yesterday she'd been slamming doors, rapping along to Cardi B, and begging him for rides to the mall. Now she was eighteen, applying for financial aid, on her way to working in a high-class medical lab. Solid paycheck, retirement, the works. He was proud of her—the better López. *At least one of us has a shot.*

"Good," Diego said. "No hanging around Brandon and his fuckin' friends. Focus on your classes, hermanita. Don't be stupid, all right?"

"What, like you?" she teased and stuck her tongue between her teeth.

"Yeah, like me. Mamá's got one fuckup to deal with. Give her two, and she'll skin us both."

"C'mon, Diego, you're not—"

"*Ah!*" He cut her off with a sharp hiss. "Don't be makin' excuses for nobody. Not me, not yourself."

"All right, all right," she said, holding the phone close to her mouth. "When'll you be home?"

"Soon. I might have a job lined up though."

"You? *Work*? Like, an actual job?"

"Hey—cállate. Cross your fingers."

"Fingers and toes."

"Te quiero."

"Love you too. Bye." She waved at the camera, and the screen went dark.

Diego stuffed the phone into his front pocket and stared at the stained-glass windows. Colorful shards beamed across the walls and hovered over the newly laid floor, giving the space an old-world charm.

Earlier that morning, he'd woken with his face tucked beneath Ariel's chin, cocooned by wings, held close by four arms. The feathers on his skull had returned, and three eyes had peeled open to look at him. Diego had touched his broad nose and traced the opening on his cheek. He'd pressed his finger to the sharp teeth behind his incisors and tried not to look disappointed when Ariel excused himself to the bathroom.

Afterward, when Ariel was black-haired and human-appearing again, they'd scrubbed the remaining graffiti off the doorframes, nailed the broken furniture back together, rolled matte white paint onto the walls, and peeled blue tape from the baseboards.

La Catedral de Nuestra Señora de Guadalupe was remade, and Diego López was left with a choice.

Stay. Go. Take the job. Start over in Austin.

He heaved an exhausted sigh and scrubbed his palm over his mouth, staring at the vaulted ceiling. Last night changed everything—*everything*—and he had no idea what to do.

"Estás bem?"

47

Diego followed the sound. Ariel stood in the mouth of the hallway, arms folded casually across his chest, shoulder propped against the frame.

"I don't know Portuguese," Diego said, which was true, he didn't. Still, the languages were similar, and he understood what Ariel had asked.

Ariel arched an eyebrow, waiting.

"Yeah, I'm fine. Just catching up with my sister."

"And how is she?"

"Good," he said and mouthed the word a second time. *Good.* "Careful." He nodded toward the bright white wall. "You'll ruin your shirt."

"It's dry." Ariel knocked on the wall with his fist. His eyes were warm, as always, searching and curious. "Would you like to go to the market with me? We can get dinner while we're there."

Over the course of two weeks, their relationship had changed. Transitioned into something more intimate, less abrasive. More blatant, less secretive. But hours ago, after Diego had spent the night worshipping at Ariel's feet, wrapped securely in his wings, he hadn't been kissed. Hadn't been touched again. Ariel had barely spoken to him. Hardly looked at him. Diego twisted his fingers together in his lap and nodded, thinking about saying *No*, saying *I should go*, saying *Thank you for the opportunity.*

But instead, he said, "Yeah, I'm starving." Because he was. God, he was.

The aura around Ariel gleamed like a second skin. His lips turned at the corners. "Me too."

The Luna County night market occupied the parking lot of an abandoned shopping center. Boarded windows and burned-out signs decorated the dusty, unmanned shopfronts, supplying an ugly backdrop for the market. Faerie lights stretched between easy-ups, and pungent smoke drifted through the air, mingling with the smell of hot peppers, grilled meat, and halved lemons. Picnic tables and plastic chairs sat arranged around busy food trucks. Vendors hollered and people chatted, drifting between booths, filling reusable bags and woven baskets with spices, clothes, fruits, and candles.

Diego bumped his shoulder against Ariel as they walked, dipping between clustered families and rambunctious children. Nearby, someone shouted 'mango, manzanas, limón,' and in the distance, cackling laughter careened over the crowd from the other side of the market. It'd been a while since Diego had been surrounded by brown skin and recipes he knew by heart, even longer since he hadn't felt the need to look over his shoulder in a crowded place and scan the adjacent areas for ICE, confederate flags, or red hats. A woman selling handmade tunics held a miniature fan in front of her face and smiled as they walked by. An old man spooned jiggly flan into his mouth and kicked off his sandal to scratch the Labrador asleep by his feet. Kids ate ice cream and churros and kettle corn. Diego breathed easily.

Ariel took his hand. "There's a Brazilian truck," he said hopefully. "I don't know if you like croquettes or stew—"

"I'll try anything once," Diego said, thrilled to have Ariel's palm clasped around his own. "I've tried a few Brazilian rice dishes at, like, fusion restaurants, but you know..." He shrugged. "That's not exactly the real deal."

"C'mon." Ariel tugged him through the bustling market, past a makeshift altar overflowing with prayer candles, flowers, and tequila bottles, and through a shadowy tent where men puffed cigars and sipped canned beer. Behind the tent, on the outskirts of the market, idled a pink food truck called Sweetfin.

They ordered cheese coxinha, spicy moqueca, and passionfruit sodas, and sat at a picnic table adorned with cardboard coasters. The coxinha—croquettes stuffed with white cheese and shredded chicken—crunched under Diego's teeth, and Ariel watched intently as he spooned fish stew into his mouth.

"It's good," Diego assured. "Really good."

"I'm glad you like it."

"So, how does...I mean, how'd you..." He paused, sipping the moqueca to buy some time. "You're Brazilian, right? Did you choose to be Brazilian or were you, I don't know, *given* this body...?"

Ariel blinked, considering. He tilted his head back and forth and struggled to find an explanation. His lips parted, but no sound followed, and he furrowed his brow, squinting at the sky before he finally spoke. "I landed here as little more than what you saw last night.

49

My true form is less cohesive. You wouldn't understand if you saw it—close your mouth, I'm not finished. I'm not saying you don't have the depth to understand; we were just created that way. To be unimaginable. But I adapted, like we all did. The world grew up around me, and I found myself circling back to Brazil. Building a life there, in Bahia, several times over. I lived in Portugal too. Spain, Italy, Guatemala, Indonesia. But Brazil was always home."

Diego nodded. He understood it on an evolutionary level: being born one thing and becoming something else, making a home somewhere new. It was in his DNA. Uprooting, settling, transitioning. "I'd like to go, someday."

"To Brazil?"

"Yeah. Everywhere, honestly."

"You will."

"You might be the only person who believes that."

"Do you believe it?" Ariel asked. He bit the last croquette in half and handed the rest to Diego.

He ate slowly, thinking about the concrete cell he'd paced around for hours, the disappointment on his mother's face, his sister rolling her eyes, and how his father hadn't been surprised. Twenty-one with a record. No college. A three-line résumé. "I don't know— I don't even have a passport."

"Well, you're the only one who needs to have faith." Ariel scraped the bottom of his bowl and licked cilantro from the spoon. "In yourself, specifically."

"I wish it was that simple," Diego said.

"You need to learn how to be gentle with yourself."

"Gentleness won't get me anywhere," he mumbled and set his elbows on the table, cradling his chin on the heel of his palm. He smiled despite himself. "Money will."

Ariel sighed, mouth ticking into a crooked smile. "Maybe you're right. Do you want something sweet before we head back?"

Diego met Ariel's earthy-brown eyes, searching for something he'd missed. A hidden message, maybe. The subject shift jostled him, but he gave a curt nod. "Sure, yeah."

Ariel stood and walked back to the Sweetfin window. Diego peeled the label off of his glass soda bottle, digging his thumbnail into the gluey paper. He imagined a life in Austin again, bartending in a big city. Then he pictured himself walking cobblestone streets in Prague, eating paella in Barcelona, and cutting through the jungle in Sumatra. Hope was dangerous, so he'd never given himself the chance to dream. He'd taken what he'd needed, done what he had to, made mistakes along the way. What he'd designed for himself, how he'd clawed out of an ill-fitting suit and restitched his skin in the likeness he'd always seen, always wanted, had been enough until right then. Until he gave himself permission to imagine adventure, to indulge in a fantasy.

But hadn't Ariel Azevedo been a fantasy too? And yet he was real. Flesh and blood. Touchable and corporeal.

Diego finished his soda and hiccupped on a small laugh, nodding appreciatively when Ariel set a plate between them. Fluffy frosting slathered the coconut cake, speared with two forks.

They ate together, listening to music boom from a nearby speaker. When the cake was gone and the sun was setting, Diego caught another glimpse of Ariel's angelic shape. His glimmery aura undulated—huge wings folded against his back, arms tucked into his lap, third eye settled intently on Diego. He looked regal. Like a thing too grand for reality. A creature made of legend, meant to be praised.

"Ready?" Ariel asked.

Diego turned toward the bustling market. People perused the booths, smiling and laughing, patting shoulders and hugging friends. "In a minute," he said and let the feeling wash over him. Homes left and remade, countries carried from one place to another, rituals remembered in tangled languages.

Ariel followed his gaze, watching the crowded market with kind eyes. "Whenever you're ready."

The church stood dark and new in the wilderness.

Ariel turned the key in the ignition and stared through the windshield. Diego stared, too, shifting his gaze from the refinished front-facing windows to the patched roof and clean doors. He tipped his head against the seat and glanced at Ariel. He was so steady. Posture, perfect. Expression, tender and open. Different from when they'd first met, when Ariel had been kind but distant, and Diego had been defensive and barbed. In the beginning, when Diego's misplaced fear had burned through him, he'd thought Ariel might've been a test. A way for life to say, *Look at this man, this presence, this unattainable beauty, another thing you cannot have*. He reached across the center console and touched Ariel's face, palm to stubbled cheek.

Ariel closed his eyes and nuzzled Diego's hand. His lips met heartlines and scarred knuckles, opened over thrumming pulse and highwayed veins. The old Jeep was stuffy with the windows closed, but Diego didn't mind. He unclicked his seat belt and pitched his body closer, angling Ariel toward him. The kiss was soft at first. Closemouthed and polite. It grew quickly, deepening as Diego pried at Ariel's lips, asking to be *kissed*, to be consumed. Ariel kissed like a person who hadn't done much of it, like someone still learning what they liked. He let Diego set the pace, made quiet, pleased noises as Diego licked into his mouth, and jerked against the seat belt still clasped across his torso when Diego snared his lip, biting hard.

"It's my turn to worship," the angel said, so close Diego felt the outline of each syllable against his lips.

The promise of being with Ariel again shot through him, knotting like a rope around his spine, yanking inward, sending heat spiraling between his legs. Diego got out and shut the passenger door. Telling his legs to behave, to keep him upright, he walked into the church. He inhaled sharply the moment his hips were seized and allowed Ariel to stop him in the aisle between pews.

"You are blessed," Ariel murmured, his voice amplified. He dunked his hand into the holy water and stroked Diego's face from forehead to chin, sinking two wet digits into his mouth.

Diego sucked at him, mouth framed by his thumb and pinky. His vision blurred, unfocused, and his head spun, thoughts hazed and whirling. How could he become completely undone in the span of a few seconds? How could a handful of movements cause him to writhe in his own skin? To be suddenly, gratefully overwhelmed? He hadn't realized he'd walked forward until Ariel turned him around, hadn't noticed they were near the pulpit, easing into the corner until his shoulder knocked the wall. Ariel stripped efficiently, and Diego watched his body morph, his wings unfold, his hair melt into feathers. He became holy and extravagant, filling the church with power.

"Do I have your permission?" Ariel asked, cradling Diego's face in two hands and unfastening his jeans with the other two.

"Yes," he said, already trembling, already wet. His breath hitched around a choked-off gasp.

Hands closed around Diego's waist and hoisted him onto the windowsill. Etched into the glass, Christ held his arms open, welcoming his disciples. Colored moonlight poured over naked skin. Diego touched Ariel's sternum. Traced the delicate skin around the eye on his abdomen, and spread his legs, baring himself, becoming an altar. He gazed at a miracle, at something incomprehensible. For the first time, Ariel kissed him in his angelic form. His mouth felt the same, plush and lovely, dripping down Diego's throat, teeth grazing his nipple, lips landing on his pelvis.

"I've come to pray," Ariel said, and his knees thumped the floor. "Through you," he added, breath gusting over Diego's cunt. "Into you."

Diego gripped the edge of the sill and held his breath, staring at the plumage on Ariel's skull, listening to his wings beat and ruffle. He tried to keep his eyes open, willing his focus to sharpen, but the pleasure rolling through him made it impossible.

Ariel opened his mouth over Diego's center. Licked and kissed. He was unnaturally warm, tending to Diego's clit with his tongue, lapping at him, sucking eagerly at slickened, swollen flesh. Diego let his head hang heavy, face tipped toward the ceiling, panting and moaning. It'd been a long, *long* time since anyone had treated him tenderly, had drawn out his orgasm slowly, tentatively. Even longer since he'd endured overstimulation, quivering in someone's mouth—*Ariel's mouth*—as he was taken apart, piece by piece, lick by lick, whimpering *please* and *God* and *don't stop* and *more*. Ariel held the back of Diego's knees and pushed his legs toward his chest, widening him, spreading him open.

"I *am* devout," Ariel said. His tongue circled Diego's clit, and he sucked until Diego jerked and whined. When he stood, Diego glistened on his chin. "How could I ever deny you?"

The church was awake. Dark and beautiful and unmade by their collision. Diego clung to Ariel, gripping his face with one hand and cramming the other between their bodies. One of Ariel's cocks dragged heavy and thick inside him, the other rested above, stroking his clit on every thrust. Diego gripped his second cock and kissed Ariel hard on the mouth, welcomed quiet, slow lovemaking. Diego met his three eyes, aware that many more were fixed on him, and let Ariel take his weight, gave himself over to being held. He touched his tongue to the narrow point of Ariel's elongated teeth, took shelter in the strong arms curled beneath his legs and wrapped around his middle, kissed him with a hunger he'd never experienced.

"I could worship you," Ariel whispered raggedly.

"I would let you," Diego said.

"Stay with me. *Stay*, little coyote," he said, breathing hard. "You'll be safe."

Diego surged forward and sealed their mouths together. "Because you'll keep me." He quite liked the idea of being kept.

"Because you're mine," Ariel rumbled.

Ariel carried him out of the nave and propped Diego against the shower wall, let lukewarm water rain down on them. Fucked him hard and fast while Diego cried out, eyes unfocused and pinned to the dewy ceiling, mumbling incoherently, "Por favor, más dura, no pares." After that, they tangled together in cotton sheets, and Diego found himself straddling an angel—*a fucking angel*—thanking a God he barely knew, discovering faith in damp skin and pearlescent feathers.

So many things he'd been, so many things he'd become.

Caged, kept, coyote, sinner, idol.

Diego López kissed an angel—*his angel*—until dawn pinkened on the horizon.

The first service at Catedral de Nuestra Señora de Guadalupe began at eight o'clock, sharp.

People arrived in dusty sedans and pickup trucks. Most wore Sunday best, dressed in collared shirts and ankle-length skirts, but some carried remnants of late-night shifts on their work clothes. Abuelas and parents quieted grandchildren, and tías fixed crooked ties. Hushed chatter fluttered through the nave, and Diego López stood in the corner, sipping coffee as families streamed inside and filled the pews.

Strange, standing in the aftermath of a rebuilt sanctuary. He'd thought the work wouldn't be done—couldn't be done—but there he was, watching light glint off holy water, rippling with every tap from a welcomed fingertip, and there they were, the faithful who'd come to worship, searching for a lost God in a once abandoned place.

Tomorrow, Diego would guide a group of travelers through the underground tunnel beneath the church. He'd arrange overnight stays for most and send coordinates for reunions with family or friends for the lucky few with rendezvous plans. He'd serve mole de panza with thickly sliced sourdough. Provide safe labor for people who were ready to work and direct families to housing organizations who could help them get settled. He'd pray with them too. *Reach for an angel*, he'd say with conviction, with power. *Someone is listening, someone will hear you, someone will find you.*

The double doors *clicked* shut, and Diego snuck into the very last pew, watching colored light stream across the floor where he'd knelt, and lain, and prayed.

The pastor took his place behind the pulpit and flicked open a well-loved leatherbound Bible. "Buenos días," he said. "Que Dios esté con nosotros."

The pew creaked beside him, adjusting to the weight of another body. "Amen," Ariel said and rested his hand on Diego's thigh.

Diego traced Ariel's thumb and turned toward the window, half listening as the sermon began. Decorating the glass, the Blessed Mother stood with her palms pressed together in prayer, and in the thin reflection, a glimmering wing extended from Ariel's back and stretched protectively over Diego's shoulder.

You listened, Diego thought, and smiled as Ariel kissed his knuckles. *You found me.*

PSALM 89:9

you rule over the surging sea; when its waves mount up, you still them

The Pelourinho neighborhood brightened the horizon. Square apartments painted mustard-yellow, salmon-pink, and jungle-green stacked like shoeboxes on either side of the hilly road. Seagulls perched on slanted roofs, and glossy sills framed rectangular windows, caged by decorative stone and filigree iron. Diego tipped his head toward the sky and inhaled, taking in the scent of brine and hot asphalt. Ariel's fingers fit neatly between his knuckles.

"You never told me you had a house here," Diego said, swiveling to scan the colorful buildings. Umbrellas lined the sidewalk, shading street vendors and snack stalls. It'd been one year—one entire year—since he'd walked into Catedral de Nuestra Señora de Guadalupe. Twelve months since he'd met Ariel Azevedo, refurbished a deteriorating church, and found himself tumbling into trust, worship, love with an angel.

"It's the only house I've had for longer than a natural lifetime," Ariel said. He adjusted his sunglasses and tugged Diego toward an orange townhouse with a bright teal door. "I pass the lease to my next of kin every sixty or seventy years."

"Next of kin, huh? *Mentiroso*," he teased.

Ariel clucked his tongue. "Sé amable."

The door creaked, revealing a tiled entryway and a floating staircase fixed with a live-edge banister. It was a lovely, open space. White kitchen cabinets spanned the left wall above a gas stove. Framed art sparsely decorated the brick walls, and a small, square table divided the dining area from the living room. Sheets draped the fixtures, and Diego circled the top of a votive candle with his fingertip, stepping around the coffee table to stand before a shuttered window. *No wonder Ariel kept this place*, he thought. Sunlight dappled a sheepskin rug spread in front of a floor-to-ceiling bookshelf, and dust glittered in the air as Ariel snapped the furniture coverings away.

"Leather," Diego purred, dragging his hand across the back of a buttery, caramel chair. He lifted an eyebrow. "Indulgent."

"Durable," Ariel corrected. He crossed the room and opened the shutters, pausing to press his mouth to Diego's temple. Gold spilled over the floor and caught the lid of a copper kettle seated on the stove.

He leaned closer, inhaling remnants of Ariel's cologne, faded after hours spent traveling, and noticed his own sour breath and dank skin, how the stagnant, recycled plane-air had stuck to him. He adjusted the backpack strap on his shoulder and jutted his chin toward the staircase. "Guessin' you've got a shower up there, right?"

"Yes, there's a shower. Are you hungry?"

"I could eat."

Ariel dropped his hands to Diego's waist. "We'll go out then. What're you feeling? Street food?" He swayed Diego back and forth, smiling fondly. "Beachside restaurant? Hole-in-the-wall cantina?"

"You pick," Diego murmured. He tipped his head, accepting a soft kiss and the coarse scrape of stubble. Even on his tired, travelworn legs, even with a twinge of hunger in his belly, Diego could've spent hours standing by the window with Ariel, lit by the waning sun.

"Go on." Ariel gave him a gentle push. "I'll freshen up, too."

"Shower with me," Diego dared.

He made a playful, suspicious noise and lifted a brow. "That'll delay us quite a bit, querido. Go."

Diego flashed a toothy grin and walked backward, making his way to the staircase. Much like the first floor, the second story boasted artwork and neatly arranged furniture. An oversized bed in a low-profile frame filled the center of the dimly lit room. There was a dresser and a nightstand, too. A roomy chair covered by a sheet; an altar set with religious statues and fresh candles. Diego dropped his backpack and stepped into the adjoining bathroom, glancing over the elegant vanity across from a deep tub. He sighed at the sight of a glass-walled shower at the end of the narrow room and left his clothes piled on the toilet lid, taking shelter under the spray of hot water. Last autumn, Ariel had installed a heater at the church, but it still didn't compare to the luxurious, steamy shower in his Brazilian getaway, and Diego couldn't help but think *we could stay here.*

They couldn't, of course. Leaving Catedral de Nuestra Señora de Guadalupe and the lifesaving tunnel than ran beneath it wasn't an option. But the idea still struck him, sitting underneath Diego's skin like a stubborn splinter. He caught the blurry image of movement through the fogged glass. Knew Ariel had paused in the bedroom and turned toward the shower, watching him.

After a year together, Ariel's attention still made Diego's heart run faster, beat harder.

Once the suds and grime were gone, Diego turned off the shower and stepped out, snatching a towel from the shelving unit above the toilet. "How should I dress?"

"It's winter here, but it'll still be warm. Something with sleeves, maybe. Nothing fancy," Ariel said.

They got ready together, navigating the space with efficiency and comfortability. Ariel wore straight-legged denim and a loose Henley, and he fixed his short hair with curl activator and coconut oil. Diego wore ripped dark-washed jeans and a thin sweater. He switched his silver piercing out for a small, yellow-gold ball, tightening the jewelry in his plush Cupid's bow. He snuck glances at Ariel, watching him crouch to tie his shoes. A glittery aura hinted at his wings, circled his head like a knight's helmet, and hovered around him, blinking in and out of existence. Sometimes it was still jarring, seeing him holy and ancient, waking to the brush of his feathers, being watched by many eyes. But Diego knew him—angel, beast, man—and he couldn't fathom being without him.

"You okay?" Ariel asked.

Diego blinked. "Yeah—yes, sorry. I'm fine. Are you ready?"

"I am." He stood and gestured to the staircase. "After you."

Down the stairs and on the sidewalk, Diego turned his face toward the sky, staring at the last sliver of Easter blue shying away from a fast-moving sunset. The neighborhood was still busy. Tourists checked into a getaway rental across the street, vendors heated grills on rolling carts, and sandals smacked the asphalt. Ariel fit his fingers between Diego's knuckles and tugged him gently toward the downward sloping street.

"Where are we goin'?" Diego asked.

Ariel jutted his chin toward the road winding through the neighborhood. "To the square."

In the center of the neighborhood, the basilica craned over town. Steeples reached high above chimneys and balconies. Rowdy patrons shouted inside bars and live bass kicked through the air as musicians warmed up for their post-sundown sets.

Diego didn't necessarily care where they went or what they did. He was happy—at peace, even—walking beside Ariel in the place he'd called home for so long—*lifetimes*. He was hyperaware of himself, though. Conscious of his smaller frame and border-accent, nervous about his slender hands and soft jawline. But Ariel didn't seem uneasy, and his confidence gave Diego a sense of safety he'd forgotten to prioritize. For the last twelve months, he hadn't needed to.

The street opened to a wide space where people strolled about, sipping sodas and cigarettes. A strip of sea glittered on the horizon and a plump Black woman swathed in a bright white petticoat stood in front of her food cart, dunking raw acarajés in bubbling oil. She flashed a toothy smile and waved, beckoning them with her free hand.

"We could start with croquettes, no?" Ariel asked, hopefully.

Diego squeezed his hand. "Yeah, sounds good."

They crossed the square and ordered acarajés with hot pepper sauce. Ariel spoke with the Baiana, exchanging full-lipped Portuguese and shoulder-shaking laughter. At one point, she gestured to Diego and said, "É este ele? Aye! He's handsome, Ariel. Bem feito." Her warm, dark eyes creased at the edges, and she winked before handing over their food. Heat rushed into Diego's face, but he smiled, fumbling over a clumsy attempt at Portuguese—obrigado, boa noite—and stayed close to Ariel's side as they made for an empty bench.

"Cléo took over for her grandmother a few years ago. Same square, same spot, same croquettes," Ariel said. He set the Styrofoam box on the bench between them and turned, pressing his kneecap against Diego's thigh. He dipped a crispy acarajé in the reddish sauce and offered a shy smile. "She was surprised, I think."

"Why's that?" Diego grabbed a croquette and sucked a piece of shrimp from a crack in the fried shell.

"I've never brought anyone home before. To Brazil, yes. But not here; not to this neighborhood."

"I'm the first?"

He tilted his head, considering. "You're the first Cléo's family has seen, and they've been here for... Oh, I don't know. A few generations."

"And they don't notice the immortality thing, I guess?" Diego teased. The croquette broke apart under his teeth—mashed black-eyed peas, sweet shrimp, coconut paste, smooth, spicy pepper, and masa.

Ariel's lips twitched. "Sometimes people don't question it. Sometimes it's a known thing."

A known thing. Diego nodded. He understood, somehow. The same way church was a ritual and communion was witchcraft. The same way miracles were acts of God spilled through human hands and depending on your clergy—your *people*—brujería was a gift or a curse. A known thing, wrapped in tradition. Like whispering the Rio Grande out of someone's lungs, like finding an angel in the desert.

These things just were, sometimes.

They ate quietly. Ariel relaxed into the bench and bounced his heel to the sound of nearby music, and Diego flicked his gaze around the square, taking in the colorful brick, floppy sun hats, and covered beachwear as the day bled into night. Soon, white bulbs came alive, strung between buildings and looped around pillars, and a band played lively music on a rickety stage. Doors were propped open, food orders were called out from carts and trucks, and people began spinning through the square, swinging each other around in a playful dance. Some folks linked elbows and swayed their hips, others nursed cigarettes and postured for each other. Diego had never been a part of something so casually confident before. Movement like that—dancing, playing—had always been a risk. But when Ariel stood, swatted crumbs off his palms, and returned to the bench after tossing their trash in a wastebin, he held out his hand and raised an eyebrow.

"You can dance, no?" Ariel asked.

Diego blushed furiously. "Can doesn't mean should."

He clucked his tongue and waggled his fingers. "Dance with me."

"You're serious?"

"I am."

Despite the heat rising in his core, Diego took Ariel's hand and followed him into the center of the square where people twirled and laughed. There, under the safety of night, Ariel tugged him closer and guided the pair into a solid rhythm. The music was loud and fun and mimicked the same feeling of old school mariachi and bluesy southern rock. Diego laughed and spun. Found purchase on Ariel's shoulders and leaned into him, allowing their bodies to gently collide. He swayed his hips, chased the delicate brush of Ariel's hand low, *low* on his spine, allowed his eyelids to droop and carded his hand through Ariel's hair.

Like that, they were different. The church disappeared, the tunnel disappeared, New Mexico disappeared, and Diego was suspended in the heat of something good and earned and true in a place where no one knew his name.

Ariel's stubble scraped his cheek, his breath coasted hot and damp on Diego's throat, and Diego wanted nothing more than to stay in that neighborhood, running his hands across Ariel's shoulders, catching glimpses of his strange, angelic aura, and anticipating the deep night: things they'd do to each other behind closed doors. He turned, pressed his nose against Ariel's jaw, went hot at the firm press of Ariel's hand on his ass, the intent in each movement—his thigh slotted between Diego's legs, how he led them through each step and twirl—and tried to keep his composure when the song ended. Applause rang out. Cheering filled the square. Couples either retreated for beverages or stayed, anticipating the next song. Diego grinned as Ariel followed him deeper into the crowd. When the music kicked up, the pair danced through another melody.

Afterward, Ariel dragged Diego into a bar where they drained skunky beers and munched on cassava chips and cheese bread. They bounced through the square as the sky blackened, pausing for specialty cocktails in a high-class tavern, and making their way to a dark, neon-lit nightclub at the bottom of a concrete staircase. The small, crowded dive thrummed with electronica, and Ariel seemed wildly out of the place. Diego laughed at first, taken aback by the sheer audacity of an angel—*his fucking angel*—bopping around with partygoers and tourists. But Ariel wasn't fazed. His hungry eyes followed each step Diego took, and once they were trapped on another dance-floor, hidden in shadow, Diego couldn't resist kissing him. Tasting mezcal on his tongue. Grinding sensually against his hipbone and moaning into his mouth. It didn't take long for Ariel to grope him over his clothes, and when they were too caught up, too lust-drunk to stay under the strobe lights, Ariel crowded Diego against a wall and kept them blanketed in shadow. He pinned Diego there, Ariel's chest to his back, Diego's ass snug between his thighs, and forced one of Diego's hands against the wall.

"You're wet," Ariel said, and slid his palm into Diego's pants, slipping his fingers between dewy folds.

"Of-fucking-course I am," Diego panted out. He angled himself closer to the wall, concealing their very public act, and rolled his hips. "You're hard."

"Should we go?"

"That or…" Diego swallowed hard. He wanted Ariel to keep touching him. Wanted to come apart with bass rattling his chest, still clothed, in front of everyone. "Don't stop, okay?" He gripped Ariel's wrist and pushed. Deft fingers framed his clit, slipped lower, curled and penetrated. Diego squeezed his eyes shut. "Keep going."

Ariel hummed against his ear, a primal sound. "I could have you." He reached deeper, stroking Diego's front wall. "I could take you in the bathroom or behind the building. I could take you here, now, if I wanted." He sealed the heel of his palm against Diego's swollen clit and pumped his fingers fast and hard. "Would you let me?"

Diego nodded. He had nowhere to hide his face, nothing to use as a shield. He came with his mouth open, trembling and gasping, and it took everything inside him not to make a sound. Around them, people danced and drank, talked and laughed. Another couple made out against the adjacent wall, and a girl shyly looked away when Diego found the nerve to see if anyone had been watching.

Before the blood could rush back into his legs, Ariel removed his hand and looped his arm around Diego's waist, hauling him toward the exit. *Jesus.* Diego's head spun. He tripped over his own feet and trudged beside Ariel, unsure of their destination until he saw the teal door.

Ariel said nothing. He unlocked the townhouse, stepped inside, and started yanking at Diego's clothes.

Kiss me. Diego made a wounded noise and did what he'd learned to do when it came to Ariel—grabbed his jaw and brought their lips together. Told him kiss me with his body, gave instructions through physicality. Ariel obeyed, prying roughly at Diego's slack mouth, and crowded him backward into the living room. Clothes fell by their feet. Diego almost tripped getting out of his jeans and laughed into another kiss. Felt the elongated points of Ariel's angelic teeth with his tongue. Heard feathers rustle, metal whirl, the air make room for antiquity.

Like this, Ariel was bigger, stronger. When he gripped Diego's waist and guided his knees onto the couch, Diego noticed how much skin his palms covered. Noticed the size of him—four-armed, hooved, and winged—caging him effortlessly against the leather. And when he looked over his shoulder, he saw eyes. All of them, open and charged, pupils blown between pale feathers and seated on Ariel's navel, aggressively fixed on him.

"You're everything," Ariel rasped, a thousand versions of his voice sounding at once. He prepped Diego with oily fingers, stretching him in a rushed, animalistic fashion. Held onto Diego's ribcage with two hands and spread him with the other two. "Tell me you know that."

"I know," Diego murmured. The confession wasn't exactly true, but it was honest enough. Ariel made him feel like he was everything. Like he was worthy. His body was on fire. His groin sparked and sizzled, and alcohol burned through his veins, loosening his muscles. Even so, he winced, bracing as Ariel positioned himself and pushed, filling him. "You don't..." He gripped the back of the couch. "You don't have to baby me. I'm fine, I'm—" He sucked in a sharp breath, suddenly seized by the throat. Ariel curled one hand around his neck, laid another over his chest, and gripped his waist, holding him steady. Drunk, he thought, but he still nodded. "I'm good. Be... Be rough."

"Are you *good*, little coyote?" Ariel purred. Playfulness snuck into his celestial voice, and he spread his wings, shadowing them in the dark room.

Diego didn't respond. Couldn't, really. Ariel set a punishing pace. His hold on Diego was iron-tight, and he worked his cocks painfully deep. Diego felt smaller than he usually did. Taken. Completely immersed and subdued. His cunt squeezed and leaked, and he let a shaky, boyish moan topple out of his slack mouth. Something shaped like a name, quiet and desperate—*please* and *Ariel*—again and again. He wanted to fold over the couch and bare himself, but Ariel wouldn't allow it. He held Diego upright, clutching his throat, fucking him brutally on the expensive furniture. Their skin met, clapping through the empty townhome, and Diego remembered to breathe, to go limp and welcome it. That overwhelming pleasure. That bliss that came with submission. His body opened for Ariel like it always did, like it'd been trained to do, and he closed his eyes as Ariel ground in deep, *deeper*.

Diego's orgasm rolled through him, steadier than the last, igniting in each limb, coiling tight in his gut. He went rigid. Tightened and contracted and spasmed. Everything brightened; everything released. At that, Ariel snapped his hips harder, fucked him in earnest, and followed suit, holding him tightly, keeping him still, emptying. Ariel grunted and rumbled. Gave tiny, aborted thrusts despite being buried to the hilt, hips flush against Diego's reddened ass, and momentarily tightened his grip on Diego's slender throat, putting the slightest pressure on his delicate windpipe.

Dios mío. Diego's lashes fluttered. He remembered to breathe. Shook and sighed when Ariel nuzzled his nape.

"Easy," Diego whispered.

Ariel loosened his grip. "Lo siento." He dropped his forehead onto Diego's shoulder and inched backward. "Bien?"

"Yeah, I'm fine. Easy," he gasped out, bracing as Ariel withdrew. If Ariel hadn't caught him, Diego would've crumbled onto the couch. "Okay, maybe..." He nodded as if to convince himself. "Maybe carry me."

Ariel folded his wings around Diego's small, spent body and repositioned him, lifting him into his arms. Like that, with limbs curved around him, Diego leaned into Ariel's chest and caught his breath, listening to the angel's strong, steady heartbeat.

"I'll run us a bath," Ariel said. He pressed his lips to Diego's forehead. "You like it here, don't you?"

"I love it here," Diego said, sighing through it.

"Maybe one day we'll make it ours. After we've handled the church... When we've passed the torch, so to speak."

Diego tilted his head back and stared at the crown of pearlescent feathers on Ariel's skull, his split cheeks, third eye... How absolute he was. How final. "One day," he said, nodding.

"One day." Ariel carried him upstairs.

FIN.

Acarajé Recipe

- Two Whole Onions
- Two Teaspoons Chile Powder and/or Dried/Crushed Hatch Chile
- 1 ½ Cup Shrimp (shelled and de-veined)
- 2 Tablespoons of Olive Oil
- 1 Teaspoon Coarse Black Pepper
- 1 Teaspoon Salt
- Canned or Hydrated Black-eyed Peas
- 1 Garlic Clove
- Fresh Jalapeño
- 2 Tablespoons Flour (for about 10 fritters)
- Olive Oil and/or Coconut Oil (for frying)

For the Filling: Slice one onion into thin bits and place them in the skillet with your olive oil. Sprinkle with salt and chile powder (or crushed hatch) and cook on a low heat until they begin to wilt and brown. This usually takes 9 – 11 minutes.

Add the shrimp and sauté with your onions until the meat pinkens. Remove from heat and season again with salt and pepper. Set your shrimp mixture aside.

Making the Croquettes/Fritters: Drain your black-eyed peas/wash canned black-eyed peas and mash them with a mortar and pestle. Chop the second onion (fully) and mince your garlic and add both ingredients to the peas.

Remove seeds from the jalapeño and finely chop.

Blend the entire mixture (all ingredients) until everything is well mixed.

Slowly add in the flour and stir until the mixture will take a nice shape. Divide the thick batter into 8 – 10 pieces and shape (rolling between palms) into balls.

Fry in a skillet with olive or coconut oil, or fry in a deep fryer, or fry in an air fryer. Make sure fritters are properly browned on all sides.

Can be served with avocado, salsa, or red pepper sauce. Top with fresh onion, cilantro, and a cooked shrimp.

Freydís Moon (they/él/ella) is a nonbinary author, poet, and mystic. When they aren't writing or divining, Freydís is usually trying their hand at a recommended recipe, practicing a new language, or browsing their local bookstore. As reflected in their eclectic catalog, they're a fan of horror, romance, sexuality, theology, and gender studies, and challenge themself to push the boundaries of acceptability and depravity.

You can connect with them @freydis_moon on Twitter.

Acknowledgements

I'm extraordinarily grateful to have built this novelette from a mere idea to a published piece. Guided by friends, early readers, and inspirational peers—Aveda Vice, R.M. Virtues, Elle Porter, Eli, Jen, Hester Steel, Magen Cubed, Harley Laroux, DC Guevara—and my editorial team at NineStar Press, I've been allowed the privilege to make my work available to readers everywhere. This little book is a dream come true.

Special thanks to my illustrator, Charbonnier Léa, who designed the beautiful special edition paperback for EXODUS 20:3. Her work can be found at: https://leacharbonnier.art

Soy Freydís. Estoy aqui para quedarme. Gracias, mi gente.